It's him, Angie thought. It's got to be him.

At last Angie watched the dark-haired man leave the establishment. She quickly followed behind him. A cold drizzle had begun to fall. "Montano," she called. "Paden Montano."

He paused on the boardwalk and slowly turned around. A wary curiosity lighted his dark eyes.

Angie smiled. It was him all right. Slipping in between buildings and under an awning, she beckoned him into the darkness. When he stepped forward, she threw off the gray hood that had covered her blond hair.

"Angie?" His voice was but a whisper, and his face seemed a mask of incredulity.

"Remember me? You and Pastor Luke saved my life by staging my escape from Silverstone, Arizona, about six years ago."

"I remember you." He glanced at the saloon building, then back at her. "And after all that trouble," he said with an obviously clenched jaw, "you return to the lifestyle we sought to deliver you from?"

ANDREA BOESHAAR was born and raised in Milwaukee, Wisconsin. Married for twenty years, she and her husband, Daniel, have three adult sons. Andrea has been writing for over thirteen years, but writing exclusively for the Christian market for six. Writing is something she loves to share, as well as help others develop.

HEARTSONG PRESENTS

Books under the pen name Andrea Shaar
HP79—An Unwilling Warrior

Books by Andrea Boeshaar
HP188—An Uncertain Heart
HP238—Annie's Song
HP270—Promise Me Forever
HP279—An Unexpected Love
HP301—Second Time Around
HP342—The Haven of Rest
HP359—An Undaunted Faith
HP381—Southern Sympathies
HP401—Castle in the Clouds

An Unmasked Heart

Andrea Boeshaar

Heartsong Presents

To my faithful readers. Where would this writer be without you? Thank you for your cards and letters of encouragement. They are precious to me.

This story, *An Unmasked Heart,* is the last in my historical *McCabe Legacy* series. I hope you will enjoy reading it as much as I enjoyed writing it. I pray this, and all the others, *An Unwilling Warrior, An Uncertain Heart, An Unexpected Love,* and *An Undaunted Faith,* will be a blessing to you for years to come. I look forward to writing a new historical series some time in the future.

A note from the author:
I love to hear from my readers! You may correspond with me by writing:

Andrea Boeshaar
Author Relations
PO Box 719
Uhrichsville, OH 44683

ISBN 1-58660-202-0

AN UNMASKED HEART

All Scripture quotations are taken from the King James Version of the Bible.

Cover illustration by Lorraine Bush.

PRINTED IN THE U.S.A.

one

California, 1873

The scene unfolding before her eyes was one Angelique Huntington had always tried to avoid when coming down to San Francisco's roughest district. Cigar smoke, like fog rolling in from the bay, swirled around the ceiling as the two gamblers faced each other. Their anxious hands twitched above their holsters, and Angie tried to sink deeper into the shadows of the Mad Dog Saloon. She'd been on her way out when she happened upon this most unfortunate encounter.

"Don't do it, you fool," a third man warned an angry-looking card player. "You draw on this fellow, and he'll kill you. Don't you know who this is?"

"Sure, I know," the first man slurred. "You just tol' me."

"Then use your head, Boy! You're in no shape for dueling tonight."

In reply, he swayed slightly and finger-combed his dirty blond hair off his forehead. He seemed to be rethinking his intentions.

Staring on, Angie pulled her dark, woolen cape more tightly around herself as the negotiator turned to address the second gunfighter. From her vantage point all she could see was the challenged man's back, his short, ebony hair, black shirt and trousers, and the bullet-laden gun belt strapped around his narrow hips.

"Please accept my apologies on behalf of my friend here, Mr. Montano," the peacemaker stated, perspiration dotting his balding head. "My friend has had too much to drink tonight, and he's always been a sore loser."

Montano? Angie perked up. She knew that name. How could she ever forget it?

"*Sí*, all is forgiven," Montano said in a deep, velvety-steel voice that held a hint of a Mexican accent. "But I suggest you take your friend home before he gets himself killed."

It's him, Angie thought. *It's got to be him.*

Slapping on his wide-brimmed hat, the intercessor grabbed hold of his blond crony and pushed him out the swinging saloon doors. Angie backed up into the corner by the staircase, praying she wouldn't be noticed. Then she regarded the man called Montano as he donned his hat and turned his back on the winnings. The raucous piano music resumed and the other patrons, some with painted-faced harlots in their laps, continued with their profane diversions.

At last Angie watched the dark-haired man leave the establishment. She quickly followed behind him. A cold drizzle had begun to fall. "Montano," she called. "Paden Montano."

He paused on the boardwalk and slowly turned around. A wary curiosity lighted his dark eyes.

Angie smiled. It was him all right. Slipping in between buildings and under an awning, she beckoned him into the darkness. When he stepped forward, she threw off the gray hood that had covered her blond hair.

"Sheriff? It's me. Angie Brown. . .except my last name is Huntington now."

"Angie?" His voice was but a whisper, and his face seemed a mask of incredulity.

"Remember me? You and Pastor Luke saved my life by staging my escape from Silverstone, Arizona, about six years ago."

"I remember you." He glanced at the saloon building, then back at her.

Angie smiled, but in the next moment her eyes grew wide as Montano seized her upper arms and shook her until she thought her brain would rattle loose.

"And after all that trouble," he said with an obviously clenched jaw, "you return to the lifestyle we sought to deliver you from?"

"No, no. . .you. . .have it. . .all wrong," she said. "Please stop. Let me explain."

He released her none too gently, and Angie swallowed hard. "Sheriff," she said, feeling irritated, "I don't recall you ever being so quick-tempered."

"Then maybe it's a good thing I am no longer a sheriff. Now you have one minute to explain before I throttle you."

Angie gulped, knowing Paden Montano didn't make idle threats.

"Remember Bethany?" she began. "The young woman who was engaged to Pastor Luke back in Silverstone? Well, she reached out to me and shared her faith while I was a. . .a working girl, so periodically I do the same here in San Francisco. I come down here to tell these women that there is a better life awaiting them if they'll only trust Christ with their souls as well as their vocations. I'm a proprietress of a dress shop along with my stepsister, Veronica." Having stated the latter, Angie couldn't help raising her chin proudly. "The Lord has been good to me."

A small chuckle emanated from the darkly clad man before her. "My apologies. . ." He gave her a polite bow. "What did you say your last name is now? Huntington? I assume that's *Mrs*. Huntington?"

"Once more, you assume incorrectly, *Mr.* Montano," Angie quipped, feeling more at ease. "After Veronica took me in, I wanted a new last name to go with my new life so no one from my past would ever find me—accidentally or otherwise. Veronica decided that I should be introduced to San Francisco society as a distant relative on her deceased husband's side, and she very graciously shared her last name with me. Together, we operate the Huntington House Dress Shop."

"I stand corrected. Forgive me."

"Of course." Angie tipped her head and grinned. From the dimly lit street behind them, she could just barely make out Montano's swarthy features. "I can tell you haven't changed a whit. Same black mustache, same penchant for saloons, card games, gunfights. . .and black clothing." She paused, lifting a brow. "Except you're wearing your hair much shorter these days."

"*Sí*, you are right on that account, but you are wrong on all others." There was a grin in his voice. "I have changed. How could I not, living in the same town as Pastor Luke McCabe? He is a most convincing preacher. I became a Christian a few years back."

"Oh, that's wonderful." Angie's heart soared at the news. "I've prayed for you. . .for everyone in Silverstone."

"We have prayed for you, too." Montano glanced over his shoulder. "May I escort you home, Miz Huntington?"

"Yes, I'd like that, but. . ." She paused, nibbling her lower lip in consternation. "But if you're a born again believer, why were you gambling in a saloon—one that exploits women in such a wicked manner?"

"Because it is, unfortunately, a part of my job, Angie," he said in hushed seriousness, but reverting, nonetheless, to the familiarity they'd shared in years past. Taking her elbow, he guided her toward a nearby hackney. She told him her address and Paden called instructions to the hired driver.

Settling into the black leather seat, Angie watched as he sat down across from her. "What sort of business are you in?" she couldn't help asking.

"I don't recall you ever being so inquisitive."

She smiled her embarrassment, but felt oddly hurt at his mocking reply. She had shared her occupation with him. In fact, he'd demanded it! Silence filled the carriage as they rode the distance to Angie's home in the South Park district. After they'd jerked to a halt, she invited Paden in to meet her stepsister. "I've told Veronica all about you over the years."

"Perhaps another time," he said. His voice sounded almost tender.

"Will there ever be another time?" she asked boldly. "There are so many questions I want to ask you."

"Such as?" She saw his mustache twitch amusedly.

"Well, I'd like to know how Bethany is faring for one thing. How are the girls at Chicago Joe's? I find myself thinking of some of them. . .praying for them."

"Many of Chicago Joe's working girls accepted the Lord and found honorable employment in other cities. Chicago Joe went out of business in Silverstone, thanks to Pastor Luke." Paden grinned. "As for Bethany, she and the pastor married and the last I saw them, some two years ago, they had quite a collection of children."

"I'm very happy for them," Angie replied, unable to suppress the note of wistfulness as Paden helped her alight from the coach. "Thank you for passing all the good news on to me."

"My pleasure. *Buenos noches, señorita.*"

His tone now held a distinct note of finality, which, Angie told herself, was of no consequence to her, so she gave Paden a parting smile and climbed the steps to the front porch. Behind her, she heard the rhythmical clip-clop of horse hooves, echoing on the brick-lined street as the carriage drove away.

❧

Lord, I need a new profession, Paden silently prayed as the carriage rocked back and forth on its way to the Oriental Hotel. When Angie had questioned his faith earlier because of where she'd seen him—and with whom she had seen him—it fueled that nagging spark of shame Paden continually carried deep within his soul. His work often took him into dens of iniquity, and he knew it wasn't right to frequent them for the sake of gleaning information; but if he quit his job with Allan Pinkerton, what else could he do? He was, after all, one of the detective agency's most capable manhunters.

A vision of the lush, wide-open spaces he'd seen in northern Texas drifted across his mind. A ranch to call his own. . . yes, that would be nice. So why didn't he just quit this business and stake his claim?

Paden ruefully shook his head. He knew the reason. As always, another Pinkerton assignment would come his way and keep him busy. Too busy to dream. But it was time to settle down. Paden sensed it now as never before. He had to quit this line of work before he caught a bullet in his back. Tonight one of the gamblers recognized him as the former sheriff of Silverstone. Word would soon spread that he was in town, and if anyone besides San Francisco's chief of police knew he worked for Pinkerton, he'd be a walking target.

Lord, not only do I need a new job, Paden added to his prayer, *I need Your protection.*

❧

"How did your, um, meeting go tonight?"

Angie stepped into the foyer and smiled at her stepsister, knowing Veronica didn't approve of her ministry at the brothels, but she could hardly expect a more positive response since Veronica wasn't a Christian. Very simply, she didn't understand Angie's occasional visits to the worst part of town for the purpose of sharing God's Word.

"My meeting went very well," Angie replied, her smile broadening. "One of the working girls accepted Christ." She hung up her wrap, wrinkling her nose at the pungent smell of cigar smoke. She'd have to be sure to air her clothing.

"Who was the gentleman who saw you home tonight?"

"That was Paden Montano," Angie said, walking into the parlor. "Do you recall me speaking about him and Pastor

Luke in Silverstone? They were the two men who helped me escape."

Veronica gasped and touched the cameo brooch pinned at the high neckline of her coral silk gown. "You don't say? He wasn't at one of those houses of ill-fame, now was he?"

"No, he. . .well, I'm not really sure what he was doing in that part of town tonight. In any event, Paden is no longer a sheriff and he's in San Francisco on business."

"Paden? Hm. . .I see." Wearing a troubled expression, Veronica smoothed back a lock of her honey-brown hair. "Do you think he'll keep quiet about your. . .your identity? I mean, he knows your past, Angelique," she stammered. "Do you think he'll spread it around the city and start a scandal?"

At the mere idea, a stream of terror coursed through Angie's veins. The one thing she feared above all else was that her past would somehow become public knowledge. "Paden won't say a word," Angie finally answered, praying it was so. "He's on my side. He helped me leave the sordid life I led. Besides, he's a Christian now."

"Yes, well, many a Christian has fallen from grace, if you know what I mean. Take my late husband, for example, the scoundrel." She blew out a derisive breath, then lifted a questioning brow. "Are you certain Mr. Montano can be trusted?"

"I'm as certain as I can be."

Veronica looked none too convinced; however, she didn't press the issue. "Would you care for some tea, Darling? And. . . oh! you simply must see the new pattern book I bought."

Angie nodded. "But first I'd like to change into something more comfortable. It's raining. . . ."

"Of course."

After a parting smile, Angie took the steps to her second-floor bedroom. The anxious knot in her chest began to loosen. She had nothing to fear from Paden Montano.

Or did she?

two

Angie reverently slid her fingertips across the raspberry-colored silk lying on the long working table. "Beautiful," she whispered.

"Isn't that the most incredible fabric you've ever seen?" Veronica asked from across the shop.

"Most certainly." Angie unrolled several lengths from the bolt and held it under her chin. "I believe I'd like a dress of this color. Can't you just see a polonaise trimmed with a cream eyelet?"

"Oh, splendid, Angelique. Simply splendid."

Angie smiled, mentally creating the fitted bodice and cut-away skirt that would be worn over a matching underskirt. The polonaise would indeed be, as her stepsister said, "splendid."

Glancing around the shop, Angie's heart swelled with gratitude. God had been especially good in blessing her with this partnership. Veronica was the businesswoman and Angie the dressmaker. Together they were a successful team, serving only San Francisco's elite.

Against the far wall hung gowns in different sizes and a rainbow of colors—all Angie's handiwork. Women's "delicates" were kept in the back room and out of the sight of any gentleman who might step into the boutique, looking for a gift, like a lace handkerchief, an exquisite shawl, or a silk scarf for the woman in his life. Of course, Angie kept busy with special orders, too, such as trousseaus.

She refolded the pinkish-red cloth and pivoted. At the other end of the store, near the front door, stood a round, polished oak table bearing several pattern books. Two comfortable armchairs were positioned beside it. Presently, Veronica busied herself with straightening the ivory lace curtains that framed the plate window. She glanced outside before looking over her shoulder at Angie. "Here he comes."

"Who?" Angie frowned. "You don't mean Captain Witherspoon."

"The very one. He's heading straight for our shop."

"Oh, my. . . ."

Angie's heart began to flutter in anxious excitement. Captain Garrett Witherspoon could turn any woman's head. He turned Angie's. Tall, broad-shouldered, with thick brown hair and serious hazel eyes, he made a handsome sight. Coupled with the fact that he was a capable sailor who traveled the world over, he proved an interesting conversationalist—one whom Angie could listen to for hours. Best of all, Garrett professed Christ and said he came from a long line of English believers who had immigrated to Maine after the Revolutionary War. Someday, he had told Angie, he meant to settle down on his family's land near the Atlantic. After he'd spoken those words, a certain light had entered his greenish-brown gaze, one that let Angie know the good captain had intentions of settling down with *her!*

But therein lay the problem, not that Angie wouldn't mind becoming Mrs. Garrett Witherspoon one day; however, she feared his family would somehow discover her less than pristine background. Most of all, what would Garrett say when he found out he'd married his own Mary Magdalene? Would he understand? Would he love her all the more for it? Or would he eye her with contempt for the rest of their wedded days?

Angie knew she should tell him about her past herself, but a knot seemed to lodge in her heart each time she considered it. What would she ever do if Garrett ended his pursuit of her and sullied her reputation around San Francisco—or around the world? She'd be ruined a second time in her twenty-five years. Once had been enough. It would be far better to forestall their budding romance now.

"Shall I make your excuses?" Veronica asked as if divining Angie's tumultuous thoughts.

"Yes, perhaps you should."

With that, Angie made her way into the back room where she touched her finger to her lips, motioning Mr. Lee, their hired Chinese security aid, to silence. He nodded agreeably and, once she felt satisfied that he wouldn't give away her whereabouts, Angie poured a cup of tea. When the tiny bell on the front door jangled, she strained to listen to the conversation between Garrett and her stepsister.

"Why, Captain, how nice to see you again."

"Thank you, Mrs. Huntington," came the resonant reply. "I wondered if Angelique is here."

"I'm sorry, but you just missed her."

"What a shame."

There was no mistaking the disappointment in Garrett's voice, and remorse filled Angie's being. She hated having any part of deceit. Moreover, she longed to have a husband and children someday, but it seemed her dream would never come true—not with her kind of history.

"I purchased four tickets to the theater tonight. There's a reception afterward, and I had hoped Angelique would accompany me. You, too, Mrs. Huntington. . .along with a cousin of mine. He just arrived in town."

"He?" Angie heard Veronica's chuckle of discomfiture. "Well, I. . .I don't know. That is, I don't care to be socially thrust into the company of a man whom I've never met."

"Pardon me, Madam, but I meant no such thing. I simply thought it would make for a pleasant evening."

"Hm. . .and what performance is it?"

"Shakespeare's *Twelfth Night.*"

"Really? I adore Shakespearean comedies."

Angie nearly dropped her porcelain teacup. Was Veronica actually considering Garrett's offer?

Peeking out the curtained doorway, she saw the back of Garrett's wide shoulders beneath his navy blue wool coat as well as Veronica's contemplative expression. In truth, Angie had always thought her stepsister would make a perfect match for the dashing sea captain. Veronica's delicate, creamy features seemed to compliment Garrett's masculine ones; she was every bit as comely as he was handsome.

"I suppose we could accompany you and your cousin to the theater after all," Veronica stated at last, much to Angie's chagrin. She didn't want to go. The more time she spent around the captain, the more she fostered a hope in her heart that would likely end in tragedy. *Romeo and Juliet might be a more fitting production for this evening,* she thought wryly.

Veronica cleared her throat. "I'll inform Angelique. I'm sure she'll be thrilled."

"I'm hoping so," Garrett replied, and Angie noted the optimism in his tone. "We'll be by to collect you ladies around six o'clock this evening."

"Angelique and I shall be waiting."

When the bell on the door signaled Garrett's departure, Angie reentered the shop. "Sister dear, what have you done?" she asked Veronica, feeling miffed. "Seems it didn't do me a lick of good to conceal my presence."

"Oh, now, don't be cross. It's just one night, and we'll get to see *Twelfth Night* free of charge. Surely you can abide the captain's company one last time." She sighed, sounding weary. "And I will have to tolerate his cousin. . .whomever that may be. I sincerely hope he's not some blackguard."

Quietly, Angie resumed her work, knowing her stepsister could spot a blackguard a mile away. Veronica's late husband had fit the bill. Angie was just too glad that Sergeant William Huntington—Billy, to most—had passed by the time she arrived in San Francisco. Not that she wished death on anyone—especially if he wasn't a believer. Simply, she'd known too many blackguards in her life to ever want to meet another.

❧

Paden couldn't help the sardonic smile that curved his lips when his cousin began describing the woman in whom he was romantically interested. She was none other than Angie Brown, also known as Angelique Huntington. Smoothing down the corners of his mustache, Paden decided this could prove to be a most uncomfortable evening since it seemed Garrett knew nothing of Angie's past.

"If she agrees to marry me," he continued, "I hope to set sail at the end of the month—with Angelique on board. I hope to beat the bad weather and make it home by Thanksgiving."

"*Sí,* I hope all turns out well for you."

"I believe Mother will take to her immediately," Garrett stated confidently before grinning at Paden from across the carriage. "You'll see. Angelique is a sweet, Christian woman. She needs a man like me to protect her."

Paden inclined his head politely, wondering if his cousin knew anything about Angie's ministry at the brothels. It seemed she could hold her own if circumstances ever warranted it. However, Paden meant to speak with Angie about her venturing into that iniquitous part of town alone. She had to stop it before she got herself killed. . .or worse.

The carriage pulled to a halt in front of the Huntington ladies' narrow clapboard house with its ornamental gingerbread trim. Paden recognized the place from when he had seen Angie home safely several nights ago. Since it seemed important to Angie, he'd meant to pay her a call and meet her sister; but in his pursuit of Harry Munson, a gunman who'd been riding with the James Gang back in Missouri, Paden had been too preoccupied for socializing.

And then he'd met up with his cousin on his mother's side: Garrett Witherspoon.

Paden's mother had been reared in an aristocratic home. Her father, Paden's grandfather, was an eccentric with interests in Mexico and on one of his many journeys there, he'd taken along his lovely daughter, who wound up falling hopelessly in love with a vaquero named Alonso Montano. Despite her father's protests, Kathleen married the charming vaquero. Paden and his four sisters were the result of their union. While the Witherspoon family conceded the marriage, it never fully accepted Paden and his father into the fold. Nonetheless, Paden and Garrett became boyhood pals during the summers when Kathleen made the long trek from Mexico to Maine to see her relatives. The last time Paden had seen Garry was at the end of this country's Civil War. They'd both enlisted with the Union.

Walking up to the porch, Garrett knocked soundly at the front door. A pretty lady with honey-brown hair and who wore a stunning lavender gown answered. She then beckoned them inside.

"Goodness, but it's cool tonight," she said, making light conversation as the men entered.

"Yes, Ma'am," Garrett replied. Then he began making the introductions. "Mrs. Veronica Huntington, allow me to introduce my cousin, Paden Montano."

"A pleasure to meet you," he said, bowing courteously. He noticed the woman's slight frown of confusion.

"Paden Montano?"

"*Sí, señora.*"

Before another word could be uttered, Angie entered the parlor, looking more beautiful than any woman had a right to. Her golden-blond hair was swept up and pinned in back with tiny ringlets hanging behind one ear. She wore a deep blue dress, which accentuated her indigo eyes, and Paden felt momentarily awestruck—until he watched Garrett stroll to her side and usher her forward. Then reality set in. Angie would soon be betrothed to a member of the Witherspoon family.

"Angelique, I should like you to meet my cousin," he said, making the introduction.

Surprise entered Angie's gaze, then she paled visibly. "Your cousin?"

Paden stifled a laugh at her horrified expression. "Miz Huntington," he said with another mannerly bow, "I'm pleased to meet you." The latter he stated emphatically so she'd understand that he had not betrayed her confidence.

She relaxed somewhat, glancing from Paden to Garrett and back to Paden again. "You're. . .related? Cousins?"

"We sure are," Garrett said, with a friendly clap on Paden's shoulder. "But our family's genealogy will have to wait. If we don't hurry, we'll miss the curtain call."

Paden gave Angie an assured wink before offering his arm to a mystified Veronica. This evening would prove to be very interesting, he decided. Very interesting, indeed.

three

Paden was aware of Angie's troubled expression throughout the play and even afterward as the four of them sat around a small table in the opulent lobby of the theater, sipping punch and enjoying some cake. He noticed Angie didn't touch her dessert.

"Now, tell me again," Veronica said, "how are you two related?"

"We're cousins," Garrett explained. "My father and Paden's mother are siblings."

"You don't look alike." Veronica studied each man's facial features.

"Very true," Garrett answered once more. "I suppose that's because Paden resembles his father, and I resemble my mother."

"Reason enough," she said lightly, giving Angie a quick glance. Then she turned to Paden. "I understand you're in San Francisco on business."

"*Sí,* that is correct."

"What sort of business are you in?"

"That's the million-dollar question," Garrett said laughingly. "No one really knows what Paden does for a living." His hazel eyes were bright with curiosity. "Some say he works for the Mexican government. Some say he works for the United States federal government. Others believe he's a bounty hunter."

"Goodness! You're quite the mystery man, aren't you, Mr. Montano?" Wearing an amused grin, Veronica looked at Garrett. "Which do you think it is, Captain?"

"Knowing my cousin, I'd say he works for whoever is paying him the largest salary. But given that Paden is a Christian now, I'm less likely to believe the bounty hunter theory."

"And you are correct. I am not a bounty hunter," Paden replied, chuckling over all the conjecture. However, he didn't offer up further explanations. Gazing across the table, he noted that Angie hadn't even cracked a smile, but peered forlornly into her glass of fruit punch.

Garrett was obviously aware of his lovely escort's dampened spirits also, and a frown of concern furrowed his brows. He shifted in his chair, appearing uncomfortable. "Perhaps it's time to call it a night. I think these dear ladies are tired."

"I believe you're right," Paden said.

The men stood. Angie and Veronica rose as well. Then Garrett offered to fetch their wraps.

Once he was out of earshot, Paden gave Angie his full attention. "Why the long face tonight? Did you not enjoy the comedy?"

She met his gaze, her eyes searching his. "How can you ask me such a question?"

"I beg your pardon?"

Veronica cleared her throat. "You have to admit, Mr. Montano, your arrival in San Francisco is quite uncanny. I'm sure if I were Angelique, I would be wondering if you came to town to warn your cousin of her past."

"Warn my cousin?" As soon as Paden grasped her meaning, he shook his head. "No, no, no. You are mistaken. Both of you." Looking at Angie once more, he added, "My cousin and I met each other by chance, I assure you. Furthermore, Garrett has no idea you and I ever met before."

Angie merely shrugged. "Well, it doesn't matter anyway."

Paden narrowed his gaze, wondering over her reply.

"Come along, Dear," Veronica said, slipping a protective arm around Angie's shoulder. She led her through the waning crowd and toward the coat check where Garrett still stood in line.

Paden marveled in their wake. Suddenly, trailing an unscrupulous outlaw from state to state seemed an easier task than figuring out a woman's mind.

❧

Angie couldn't sleep, so she felt grateful for Veronica's company as well as the chamomile tea steeping in the floral-patterned, porcelain teapot.

"Do you think Mr. Montano was lying when he said he didn't mention your past to the captain?" Veronica queried as she poured the fragrant brew.

Angie took the proffered teacup and saucer. "I've never known Paden to lie."

"Well, then, what's to fret about?"

"Nothing. . .everything!" Frustrated, Angie stood and began pacing the rose-papered room. "Oh, Veronica, I wish I didn't have to wear a mask and hope and pray that no one will find out about the woman beneath it—the woman with the despicable past."

Her stepsister gave her a sympathetic grin. "Worrying can't change a thing, so sit back down and drink some tea. After a good night's sleep, you'll feel better."

"But don't you see? Garrett is sure to propose marriage any day now. I'd love to accept, have children, live happily ever after."

"That could never happen," Veronica stated with an emphatic shake of her head. "The happily ever after part, I mean. You don't love Garrett Witherspoon."

"I love him as much as I could love any man."

"Nonsense. You're better off without him."

"But—"

"Angelique, I know what I'm saying. Marriage is. . . constraining."

"Not for Christians. You should hear how my pastor preaches on wedded bliss."

"If his wife preached on the subject, I might listen."

Veronica sipped her tea while Angie took her place in the parlor chair once more and then lifted her porcelain cup to her lips.

"You know, he is quite handsome, not to mention very charming."

"Who?" Angie asked. "Garrett?"

"No, no. . .Montano."

"Paden?"

"*Sí, señorita*," Veronica quipped.

Angie swept her gaze upward.

"He's got a very straight, aristocratic nose, and his dark eyes don't seem to miss a thing." A faraway expression crossed her face. "When he looked at me, Angelique, it was as if he could see right into my soul."

"Don't be silly."

Veronica snapped from her musing. "Silly? Is that what you called me?" She shook her honey-brown head. "I'm extremely serious. Come now, admit he's attractive."

Angie couldn't lie. "All right. I admit it. He's a nice-looking man. But he's also very rugged, accustomed to wild places. He's had to be, living in the Arizona Territory all those years. Moreover, Paden Montano is a famed gunman."

Veronica leaned forward. "How many people do you think he's killed?"

"I'm sure I wouldn't know!" Angie frowned at her stepsister's curiosity. "You're not. . .interested romantically in Paden. . .are you?"

"Of course not." Veronica moved to pour herself another cup of tea. "I lived with one cruel man already, and I'm certainly not going to get myself involved with another."

Angie mulled over the reply. "Just for the record, I don't

believe Paden is cruel," she stated at last. "He might not be the marrying kind, but he's not anything like your late husband. From what you've described, that man was downright mean."

"That's putting it mildly." Veronica paused, looking pensive. "May I ask you something extremely personal?"

Angie thought it over, deciding there wasn't much about her life, past or present, that her stepsister didn't already know. "Of course," she replied at last.

"Was Mr. Montano ever one of your, um, customers back in Silverstone?"

"No, never." Unbidden memories surfaced and Angie recalled the handsome, much sought after sheriff. Chicago Joe's girls had literally fought over him whenever he entered the brothel, although Paden often had a strong drink and a good card game on his mind, much to the prostitutes' disappointment.

Veronica replied with a dignified, "Hmph. I'm glad to hear it. I'd hate to think he was *that* kind of man."

"Even if he was, that part of his life is over now," Angie said. "Just as God delivered me from that horrible pit and miry clay, He saved Silverstone's former lawman. Paden said he's a Christian and, although I haven't had a chance to talk to him about it, I don't doubt his word."

"A Christian?" Veronica lifted her shoulders noncommittally. "Well, I suppose religion helps some people along." She sipped her tea, looking pensive. "You know, I'll never forget my first sight of you, standing on my doorstep, looking like a half-drowned kitten."

"I am forever indebted to you for taking me in," Angie stated sincerely.

"Indebted? Hardly. You proved yourself worthy of my attention and my home, and now we operate a thriving business together. We're friends. More than friends, we're sisters. And we're happy."

"Yes, we are. . .happy." Forging a smile, Angie brought the

teacup to her lips. She felt like a hypocrite, for the hollowness in her heart didn't mirror the placid words she'd just spoken.

She wasn't truly happy. She wanted more. She yearned for a husband to cherish and protect her. She longed for a baby to cradle in her arms, a child to nurture and love.

And the only way she'd ever attain her desires was if she married Captain Garrett Witherspoon!

four

"Angie!"

Hearing her name, she stopped on the boardwalk in front of an apothecary. She knew who had called her even before she turned around since no one in San Francisco called her "Angie."

"Good afternoon, Mr. Montano," she said in feigned formality. She still couldn't get over how different he looked without his long hair tied back at his nape with a leather band. In Silverstone, folks often remarked that Paden Montano could double as an Apache. But today, dressed in dark trousers, vest, white shirt, and black jacket, he appeared quite the refined gentleman—just as he had last night.

Holding his wide-brimmed hat in one hand, Paden grinned and gave her a courteous bow. All the while he eyed her closely, and Angie suddenly recalled what Veronica had said: *When he looked at me, Angelique, it was as if he could see right into my soul.* Yes, Paden definitely had that effect on a person.

"I wondered if I might have a few words with you," he told her now.

"Well, I am on my way to the bank—"

"May I accompany you?"

Angie shrugged. "If you'd like."

She began walking and Paden easily fell into step beside her. "You did not enjoy yourself last night," he began. "I have been wondering why."

"It's a long story, one I'm sure you don't have time for."

"On the contrary, I would like to hear it."

Angie paused in front of the bank. "Why?"

A softness entered Paden's dark eyes. "I care about you. I have what you might call a vested interest in your life, both because I helped you escape from Silverstone and because my cousin plans to make you his wife." When she inhaled sharply, Paden added, "That should not come as any surprise to you."

"I'm not surprised. . .exactly. I simply didn't expect you to be so frank."

Angie glanced around nervously, hoping passersby couldn't overhear their conversation. Just across the street, she spied one of the "mud hens," a name given to women who gambled in mining stocks and who had lost all their money. Destitute, they begged coins off the more affluent who did their business in the city's financial district, but then they gambled away their handouts. A pathetic station in life, yet Angie knew the Lord could deliver any of those poor souls. Just as He had delivered her.

Angie swung her gaze back to Paden. "You don't think I'm good enough to marry Garrett, is that it?"

"I never said that." He shook his head in obvious disappointment. "Do your banking, *mi amada*, and when you are finished, we will sit down and discuss this matter over refreshments."

"I need to get back to the dress shop."

"I think we will talk first."

Angie opened her mouth to argue, but the severe expression on Paden's face made for a change of heart. "I'll be back shortly," she said.

"*Sí,* I will be waiting."

Inside the stately, red brick building with its ceramic-tiled floors and mahogany-paneled walls, Angie headed for the teller window. She'd nearly reached it when Mr. Rosewahl, the bank's president, caught her by the elbow.

"Did that man accost you, Miss Huntington?" he asked indignantly. Although he dressed impeccably, the man always reminded Angie of a large, balding bird. "I can summon the authorities if you wish."

"Excuse me?" she asked, frowning her confusion.

"That Mexican. Outside. Did he harass you in any way?"

Giving him a reassuring smile, Angie shook her head. "That's Paden Montano. He's an acquaintance of mine, and he happens to be Captain Garrett Witherspoon's cousin."

"You don't say. . . ." Mr. Rosewahl's hawklike gaze darted to the shuttered window, opened just enough to reveal Paden's shadowy silhouette. "Montano, eh?"

"Yes, that's correct."

Mr. Rosewahl looked back at Angie. "Well, then, I guess there aren't any problems to report."

"No, Sir."

With a polite, parting smile, Angie walked the rest of the way to the window, where she made her deposit. Once the task was completed, she rejoined Paden on the boardwalk. "There's a small café up the street," she suggested. "We could talk there. I know Mrs. Tibbles serves up a fine cup of tea."

"Tea?" Paden arched dubious brows.

"Or a good, strong cup of coffee."

"*Sí,* that is more like it."

As they strolled amicably, side-by-side, Angie judged Paden's height to be no more than a few inches taller than her own five feet three inches. Garrett stood at least six feet. Regardless, Paden Montano seemed to exude the more commanding presence, even though his cousin governed numerous bawdy crewmen during his voyages. Mentally shaking herself, Angie wondered why she was even comparing the two men.

After they'd entered the café, Paden chose a quiet corner table in the far end of the sparsely occupied establishment.

Preparing to seat himself, he unbuttoned his jacket, and Angie glimpsed the wide gunbelt strapped around his waist. Once more she questioned his occupation, mulling over the choices Garrett had listed last night. Employed with either the Mexican or American government? A bounty hunter?

"So what exactly is your business, Paden?" Angie couldn't help asking.

He grinned wryly. "What do you think?"

Mrs. Tibbles's youngest daughter, Susan, a brunette with unmanageable curls tucked beneath a white scarf, came over and took their orders. Then she strolled off in the direction of the kitchen.

"I think maybe you work for the army."

"I used to."

Angie felt herself grow frustrated. "Well, unless you tell me," she challenged, "I refuse to speak to you, and we can just sit here and drink our beverages in silence."

He sniffed loudly and appeared as though he were trying not to chuckle, which made Angie all the more irritated.

Susan reappeared, set down Paden's coffee and Angie's tea, then departed.

"I can't say I mind my *silent* view," Paden said emphatically, stirring sugar into his brew. "I think I could gaze at you for hours, Angie. You've become a very beautiful woman. My cousin is a lucky man."

Angie's face warmed with embarrassment.

"Which brings me to the reason I wanted to speak with you today."

Chagrin gave way to acquiescence. "Oh, fine. What is it you'd like to know?"

"It is more like what I want you to know. I have no intentions of betraying your confidence." He lowered his voice until it was but a whisper. "I will take the secret of your past to my grave."

"How comforting," she quipped.

Looking amused, he took a long drink of his coffee.

"But the fact of the matter is, Garrett is entitled to know before he. . .he marries me."

"True. But you must be the one to tell him."

"You make it sound so simple," Angie said, tasting the bitterness of her words. She gazed into her teacup for several long moments before looking back at Paden. "How do you think Garrett will react when he discovers the news?"

"That I cannot say."

"He's your cousin. Can't you give me some idea?" She closed her eyes as several anguished heartbeats elapsed. "Paden," she began again, "what is the Witherspoon family like? Will they accept me, knowing who I am? What I was?"

"They do not have to know. This matter is between you and Garrett. Although," he added, wearing a pensive frown, "my aunt Mary will probably want you investigated."

Angie groaned.

"But take heart," Paden stated lightly, "perhaps she will hire me to do the detective work."

Angie narrowed her gaze. "You're a. . .a detective?"

"*Sí,* I am a Pinkerton agent. But I trust you will keep my secret just as I have promised to keep yours."

She nodded, oddly impressed by the admission.

"I'm here in San Francisco searching for a renegade, but I do not want the fact uncovered just yet—for obvious reasons."

"I understand. I won't say a word. Not even to Veronica."

"*Gracias.*"

"Now, back to my question about the Witherspoon family. . ." Angie took a deep stifling breath. "Do you think I'll fit in?"

"Surely my cousin has told you about his family."

"Yes. . . ."

"So the question is, do *you* think you'll fit in?"

"I. . .I don't know." She expelled a deep sigh. "I seem to

vacillate on the subject. Perhaps I should abandon the idea of marrying Garrett altogether."

"You give up so easily. Isn't your love for my cousin worth braving a few patricians?"

"My love for him?"

"*Sí.*" Paden eyed her quizzically, causing Angie to look away and concentrate on her tea. "You don't love him?"

"Well, I. . .I like him very much," she said. Then suddenly she wanted to share her innermost thoughts with Paden. She had to unburden herself to someone and Veronica certainly wasn't any help. Besides, Angie felt certain she could safely confide in the ruggedly handsome man sitting across from her. After all, they were already keeping each other's secrets. What was one more? "I'm sure after we're married I'll love him. He's a Christian. He'll provide a comfortable lifestyle for me. He's everything a woman could want in a man. Surely, love will come."

"That is a big gamble."

"Yes, but how can I possibly lose?"

❧

As Paden drank his coffee and listened to Angie's faulty reasoning for marrying Garrett, he couldn't help feeling oddly hopeful. Last night he'd lain awake in bed, staring at the darkened hotel room's ceiling. All he could think about was Miss Angie Brown—that is, Miss Angelique Huntington.

Back in Silverstone, he'd sensed something special about the disheveled girl with haunted, blue eyes. She had stood apart from the other hardened females at Chicago Joe's—which was one of the reasons he willingly risked his life to help Angie escape from that profane lifestyle. Seeing her transformation, he knew the venture had been worth it. Except, he'd seen traces of that same futility in her gaze last night, and it disturbed him enough to lose precious hours of sleep. This morning, he felt strongly that he had to speak with her. Perhaps it had been spawned from sheer male pride, but Paden had wanted to be the one to rescue her once more.

This time, from a loveless marriage.

He listened as Angie admitted to wanting a husband, a family. She told him how in the past few years, God had healed her heart, her soul, and her mind. She now knew that not all men were lascivious creatures, and through several Bible studies, she'd learned the difference between fornication and the act of intimacy after marriage. However, Angie did not come out and directly state the latter. Rather, her face turned a pretty shade of crimson as she stammered out her meaning. Even so, Paden got the gist of it.

"I'm so embarrassed," she murmured. "I mean. . .bringing up that subject."

He gave her a patient smile. "If you were not blushing, I would not believe that the Lord restored your spirit. But I can see He has."

Angie looked relieved. "Nevertheless, Garrett deserves to hear the truth."

"I agree. So what's stopping you from telling him?"

"Fear, even though I know God doesn't give us the spirit of fear. Still, I can't seem to help it." Angie finished her tea. "What if Garrettt spurns me and divulges my past to others, leaving me scandalized?"

"And you believe he might do that?"

"I don't know. I guess it all boils down to trust, doesn't it?" she said at last.

Paden nodded.

"I never realized it before, but I guess I'm afraid to trust Garrett."

"And trust is the cornerstone of a happy marriage, is it not?"

Angie arched a golden brow. "How'd you ever become so wise on the subject?"

Chuckling, Paden fingered his mustache. "I watched my

parents. Never have two people loved each other more than my mother and father."

"That's really nice," she said, looking so misty, it caused Paden to wish he could pull her into his arms, soothe her fears and worries, and replace them with—

He shook himself mentally. What in the world was he thinking? It was one thing to save a woman from marrying the wrong man, and quite the other to step in as the groom.

He considered her, watching her strawberry pink lips as she spoke. Marry Angie. The idea was tremendously appealing. His past wouldn't frighten her, just as hers didn't shock him. Together they could make a life for themselves in Texas. Build a ranch. Settle down.

"Paden, did you hear me?"

He shook himself from his reverie. "I'm sorry. What did you say?"

"I said, I have to get back to the dress shop. Veronica will be wondering why I've been gone so long."

"Of course. Allow me to escort you."

"Thank you." She smiled, and Paden's insides warmed.

Dear God, what is wrong with me? he prayed as he paid for their beverages. He wasn't a man given to whimsical thinking. He was one who knew the cold, hard, even cruel realities of life. But, perhaps, it was time to do a little dreaming. And a little courting. True, he had courted a number of ladies in the past six years. Good, decent, pretty women, but none had the certain spunk he desired. He wanted a woman who would keep his life interesting, not bore him or nag him to an early grave. That woman was Angie. He could sense it. However, difficult as it may be, he had to stay out of the way until she made up her mind about Garrett—one way or the other.

"Paden?"

He started when Angie touched his arm. Then he noticed they stood in front of the Huntington House Dress Shop.

"You seem a million miles away," she said. "Is everything all right? Did I say something to offend you?"

"No," he assured her. He wanted to reach out and caress her cheek, feel its softness beneath his palm. Instead, he jammed his hands into his jacket pockets and resisted the urge. "I'm fine. Just thinking."

Angie's indigo eyes brightened. "If everything is all right, I guess I should get back to work. Thank you for listening to me babble on about my problems."

"It was my pleasure."

She smiled briefly before her expression changed to one of earnestness. "Garrett is coming to dinner tonight. Would you. . . would you come, too? I have a feeling he's going to propose, but with you there. . .well, it might buy me some time to pray about the situation further."

Paden thought it over and couldn't see any harm in it. "Thank you for the invitation. I would be happy to accept. What time, and where?"

"Our house and. . .about seven o'clock."

"I will be there."

five

The dinner table was lavishly outfitted with Veronica's best English dishes. White plates, bowls, platters, cups and saucers, having a rose motif and gold trim, added bits of color atop the pearly tablecloth. Beyond the dining room, in the kitchen, Tu Hing, the Chinese cook, busily prepared a scrumptious-smelling fare that caused Angie's stomach to rumble in anticipation.

"It's been quite awhile since we've entertained anyone other than the Ladies' Literary Society," Veronica stated as she primped in front of the gilt-framed hall mirror. Dressed in a stylish, burgundy Gabrielle dress with white flounces, she ironically matched the rose-patterned wallpaper in the parlor and her exquisite dinnerware.

Angie grinned. "I hope you don't mind that I invited Paden."

"Not at all. In fact, it'll give me someone to talk to while you and Captain Witherspoon ogle each other."

"We do not 'ogle.' At least, I don't."

Veronica swung away from the mirror. "No, I don't suppose you do." She sighed. "Why haven't you severed this relationship, Angelique? Nothing will come of it. You said, yourself, the captain isn't likely to sympathize with your past. Why are you wasting your time. . .and his? There's no use in leading the poor man on."

Disappointment flooded Angie's being. Her stepsister's words rang true; unfortunately, Angie didn't feel quite ready to give up her dream of having a family of her own. "I. . .I'm still praying about. . .things," she stammered.

Veronica gave her a quelling look. "Angelique, I have protected you all these years. Remember the young banker who began calling on you? I put an end to that, now didn't I?"

"Yes, but that was different. Archie wasn't the man for me."

"And what about Mr. Morgan, the tailor?"

Angie wrinkled her nose in distaste. He hadn't attracted her in the least bit.

"And Mr. Parsons, Mr. Jensen, Mr. Smith. . ." Veronica counted the names on her long, tapered fingers. "Mr. Santiago, and that poor widower with all those smudge-faced brats. . ."

"I thought he rather preferred you, sister dear," Angie teased.

Veronica rolled her eyes, seemingly appalled. "My point is this—I have spared you numerous times from making a terrible mistake."

"Perhaps, but I wasn't interested in any of those other men."

"But you're interested in the captain? Still?"

Angie felt herself blush as she shrugged out a reply.

"Aren't you the least bit concerned that you'll return to your wanton ways if you're ever intimate with another man?" Veronica asked pointedly. "It's a sickness, you know."

Angie gulped down the sudden lump of revulsion rising in her throat. "No, Veronica, it's not a sickness. Not for me, anyway. What began as a state of hopelessness became a lifestyle of sin. I thought I was nothing. Nobody. I thought it was my fault your father, my stepfather, abused me after my mother died. But then a sweet little Christian schoolteacher by the name of Bethany Stafford showed me differently." Angie's voice softened, and she had to smile as she recalled her conversion experience. "Bethany said God loved me, that He created me before the beginning of time, and that He wanted me to be His child. All I had to do was—"

"Yes, yes, I've heard the rest before. You found religion." Strolling into the parlor, Veronica tossed an impatient glance over her shoulder. "For the record, my father was almost as despicable as my late husband."

Angie closed her eyes in a moment's anguish, wondering how that could be possible.

"So you see, we've both been brutalized by men. We're better off committing our lives to each other and our dress shop rather than husbands. Although, I must admit," Veronica added, peeking around the gauzy sheers and out the front window, "it is rather pleasant to be in the company of a handsome face now and then." Straightening, she looked across the room at Angie. "But the secret to happiness is remaining unmarried."

Angie nibbled her lower lip in consternation. Could her stepsister really be correct?

❧

"What are you doing here?"

Stepping up beside him on the Huntington ladies' front porch, Paden gave his cousin a sardonic grin. "I was invited."

"Oh? And might I presume Mrs. Huntington did the inviting?" Garrett asked with a conspiratorial nudge of his elbow. "She's a lovely widow, in spite of her audacious streak. Unfortunately, she's not a Christian."

"God saw fit to save me," Paden replied, "He can save anyone."

Garrett rapped on the heavy, oak door and grinned. "I can't argue with you there."

Moments later, Angie appeared in the entryway, bidding them welcome. One look at her, dressed in a lilac-colored gown, her blond hair tied back with violet ribbons, and Paden felt his mouth go dry. Next he watched in a mixture of awe and envy as his cousin took Angie's proffered hand and placed a light kiss on her fingertips.

"You're as enchanting as always, Angelique."

"You're too kind."

A blush crept up her cheeks before she glanced at Paden. He inclined his head politely.

Angie smiled. "Well, come in. Both of you. Come in."

Paden followed his cousin through the doorway and then, after Angie took their overcoats, he trailed Garrett into the parlor. There they found Veronica perched comfortably on the settee.

She smiled a greeting. "Would either of you care for a small glass of wine before dinner?"

Both men politely refused the offer. Making his way to an upholstered armchair, Paden took a seat, leaving the matching armchair for Garrett and the other half of the settee for Angie; but as it happened, Angie strolled into the room and claimed the armchair. Still standing, Garrett rubbed his jaw in uncertainty.

"Lovely weather we're having," Angie began, smoothing her satiny skirts.

"Quite." Veronica appeared amused as she obviously noted Garrett's predicament.

Paden wanted to chuckle and he almost felt sorry for his cousin. Next, he decided that in spite of her impure past, there was still an element of naiveté about Angie. Obviously the Lord had restored that quality along with her soul.

Veronica cleared her throat. "Angelique, Dear. . ." She patted the place beside her.

After a frown of confusion and a glance at Garrett, Angie's cheeks turned a lovely shade of scarlet. This time Paden couldn't contain his amusement.

"I'm so sorry, Garrett," Angie gushed as she stood. "I don't know what I was thinking. I guess I wasn't thinking at all."

"It's been a long day," Veronica said. "We were very busy at the shop this afternoon."

"Well, then, this invitation to dine with the two of you is doubly appreciated," Garrett remarked, sitting in the armchair now.

"We love to entertain, don't we, Angelique? Why, we were discussing the very subject just moments before your arrival. Isn't that right?"

Paden watched Angie nod beneath Veronica's pointed stare. Then a few moments of weighted silence passed, marked by the slow ticking of the grandfather clock, poised in the corner of the parlor.

"Captain, when do you next set sail?" Veronica asked, breaking the uncomfortable lull.

"I hope to leave by the end of the month." He gazed at Angie with a longing in his eyes that Paden didn't miss.

She quickly looked away.

"I do hope you remember your promise to bring me some of that Oriental silk I've been hearing so much about," Veronica said.

"Oh, yes, Ma'am. That is, I'll bring you the fabric if I ever make the voyage to the Orient again. You see, I plan to sail back to Maine and spend some time with my family." Once more, Garrett's eyes lingered on Angie, although she kept her gaze riveted on her hands, folded neatly in her lap. She had undoubtedly grown uncomfortable with his unspoken solicitations.

Paden fingered his mustache and continued to gauge the situation. He found it curious that his cousin behaved like an infatuated schoolboy in Angie's presence when, in fact, he was known to make seasoned crewmen cower over their disobedience.

A Chinese man, wearing a starched, white apron over black apparel, suddenly appeared in the doorway. "Dinner is served," he announced with a polite bow.

"Thank you, Mr. Hing." Veronica stood and eyed her guests. "Shall we eat?"

❧

Picking at her fish, Angie inwardly cringed at the turn in the conversation. Veronica, in her usual probing manner, had begun to question Paden about his experiences in the Arizona Territory.

"I heard those Indians are savages!" Veronica declared, forking some fried rice into her mouth.

"Many are, but many are not," Paden answered.

"Personally, I would rather confront a hurricane than one of those murdering Indians," Garrett said. "I have heard horror stories from settlers and soldiers, alike. Some of the gruesome deaths they described are—"

"Are not for ladies' ears," Paden interjected.

Garrett had the good grace to look abashed. "My apologies, Angelique. Mrs. Huntington."

"Oh, don't worry. Angelique and I are made of sturdier stuff than that. Aren't we, Dear?"

She replied with a feeble nod.

"We read the *Chronicle* every day, you know," Veronica said from her place at one end of the table. "Besides, with all the riffraff in this city it's a wonder there are any decent citizens left at all. There are gambling dens by the dozens on the waterfront, and saloons, and bordellos. . . ."

Angie felt as though she might be sick.

"Of course, I've never been near any of those horrid establishments. I'll bet you didn't have to worry about such corruption in the Territory, did you, Mr. Montano?"

"On the contrary. We had our share of problems."

"Now, in what little town did you say you were sheriff?"

"Silverstone. Silverstone, Arizona."

"Yes, that's right," Veronica said, taking a sip of her tea. "It sounds like a mining town. What do you think, Angelique?"

She slid her gaze to Veronica's, wondering if her stepsister had gone mad. What could she possibly be thinking, bringing up Silverstone?

Tu Hing entered the dining room, carrying a carafe of coffee.

Angie gave him a polite smile. She and Veronica never could get used to calling him by his first name, so they simply referred to him as Mr. Hing. She watched now as he dutifully filled the men's cups before retreating to the kitchen.

"Tell me, Mr. Montano, did you ever have any. . .adventures while you were sheriff?"

Paden grinned wryly. "*Sí,* I had a few." His eyes met Angie's from across the table and she saw pools of sympathy in their dark depths. Then he looked back at Veronica. "The territories are becoming famous for their *bandidos*, and several had the misfortune of straggling into my jurisdiction."

"Oooh, be still my heart," Veronica crooned, her hand fluttering to her chest. "If this were a novel, Mr. Montano, I'd just have to turn the page and read what comes next."

"Good thing it's real life," Angie muttered.

Sitting to Veronica's right, Garrett chuckled softly.

"Did you do anything heroic, Mr. Montano? Did you ever rescue anyone from danger?" Veronica asked emphatically.

Angie gasped, inhaling a sip of tea. Next, she proceeded to cough uncontrollably. Garrett was swift to come to her aid. When at last her choking subsided, she apologized to their guests before sending Veronica a warning glare. Her stepsister was treading on dangerous ground.

Veronica smiled back in feigned innocence. "Better now, Angelique?"

"Much," she stated, clearing her throat one last time. "Thank you."

Garrett reclaimed his chair. "Mrs. Huntington, I have a hunch Paden's life as Silverstone's sheriff was quite different than anything you might read in a dime novel."

"You think so?" Veronica turned her inquisitive, hazel eyes to Paden. "So no saving damsels in distress, hm?"

A slow smile spread across his face. "As a matter of fact, I can recall the rescue of one woman in particular."

Angie felt the blood draining from her face.

"Oh, do tell, Mr. Montano."

"She'd been captured by a band of Yuma," Angie heard Paden say over the anxiety roaring in her ears. "I had gotten to be on friendly terms with the Indians, and after three days, I managed to convince one of the braves to release the woman. She was then reunited with her husband and small children."

"How absolutely thrilling!" Veronica exclaimed. "Angelique, did you ever hear such a tale?"

"I'd rather not discuss it." Truth to tell, she'd heard sagas that would curl Veronica's honey-brown hair. But Angie would never subject her stepsister to such shocking accounts. She vehemently wished Veronica would cease her interrogation of Paden.

Lifting her linen napkin, Angie unwittingly dabbed her temples. They'd begun to throb.

"You're not coming down with one of your sick headaches, are you, Darling?" Veronica asked, her face a mask of concern.

"I'm all right."

"You do look a bit peaked," Garrett said with a troubled frown.

"Shall I get the laudanum?" Veronica asked sweetly.

Angie took several deep breaths. "I'm really fine," she assured everyone, but inside, she felt like sobbing. She hadn't escaped Silverstone; it still held her in bondage. What good was cultivating a new life if just below its surface lurked the demons from her past, ready to spring at any moment? Hadn't Veronica proved that much tonight?

"Miss Huntington?"

Paden's deep voice, spiked with its subtle Mexican accent, penetrated her tumultuous thoughts. She glanced at him expectantly.

"Perhaps a bit of air will do you some good."

"My cousin is right," Garrett said. He quickly rose from the table and helped Angie to her feet. "Some cool sea breezes will perk you right up, and I'm more than happy to accompany you. We'll stroll in the moonlight together."

Angie glimpsed the ardor shining in his brownish-green eyes and shuddered inwardly. If Garrett proposed, she knew she'd have to be completely honest with him. However, she didn't feel up to it. Not now. Not tonight. . . .

"A walk sounds pleasant enough to me," Paden said. "How about you, *Señora* Huntington?"

"Oh, well, I—"

"Good. Then it's settled." Paden pushed back his chair and stood. He grinned at Garrett's glowering countenance. "The four of us shall take a little moonlit stroll, *sí?*"

"*Sí,*" Angie replied quickly, a wave of relief pouring over her.

Making their way through the parlor, Angie paused near the front door to hand each gentleman his overcoat. As she gave Paden his, she managed to whisper, "You've been a veritable hero tonight. How will I ever thank you?"

Paden leaned forward and playfully chucked her under the chin. "Do not worry, my little *mariposa,*" he whispered back, "I will think of something."

six

The sun had long set when the group of four headed out on their stroll. Cool Pacific breezes blew wisps of Angie's hair onto her cheek and she brushed them backward. As they proceeded down one of San Francisco's many hilly, unpaved avenues, Angie gazed heavenward and found herself momentarily awestruck. The expanse of the dark sky was dotted with stars, reminding her of ivory sequins sewn onto endless yards of black velvet. *Lord,* she thought, *Your handiwork is perfect.*

Just then a passage in Psalm 8 came to mind. "*When I consider thy heavens, the work of thy fingers, the moon and the stars, which thou hast ordained; What is man, that thou art mindful of him?*"

And who am I, Angie wondered, *that the Creator of the universe would love me enough to die for my sins?*

"*Fear not,*" came God's words from the first verse in Isaiah 43, "*for I have redeemed thee, I have called thee by thy name; thou art mine.*"

I am God's, she marveled. *He called me by my name. He wanted me for His own. Me!*

It suddenly occurred to Angie that if she were good enough for God, she certainly ought to be good enough for the likes of Garrett Witherspoon. She looked at him askance, realizing he was explaining in great deal how sailors gauge the wind's velocity and how they rig up their sails accordingly.

Angie stifled a yawn.

"I have never been on a ship," Veronica said as they came up to a sandy knoll near the Golden Gate Park, which was still in the process of being developed. From their vantage point, they could see the crowded San Francisco Harbor. Beyond it was the strait called the Golden Gate. Angie could vividly recall the trepidation and excitement she felt some six years ago as the ship bringing her to San Francisco cruised into the bay.

"I prefer to sail rather than travel by stage or even the railroad," Garrett declared.

"Really? I have only traveled on a miserable wagon train," Veronica said.

Lowering herself onto a large boulder, Angie listened as her stepsister and the captain discussed the advantages of journeying by boat.

Paden pointed to the place beside her on the rock. "May I?"

Angie nodded and scooted over to make more room for him.

The conversation between Garrett and Veronica continued.

"Would you like to know another secret?" Angie whispered to Paden. He turned his head and faced her. Beneath the moonlight, she saw him grin. "I get terribly seasick."

Paden's smile broadened. "Does my cousin know that?"

Angie shook her head.

"It's a long way from San Francisco to Maine."

"So I hear."

Paden chuckled.

"Do you get seasick?"

"No, but I get very bored. Nothing but sky and water to look at for days on end. The last time I sailed on a clipper, I was seventeen. I sailed to Maine with my mother to see her family."

"Did you and Garrett get along back then?"

"Oh, *sí,* we were *amigos* from the beginning. Garry and I spent many happy summers together, causing all sorts of mischief." Paden laughed softly. "But my grandfather, aunts and uncles, and several cousins did not like me because my father is Mexican. However, over the years, their hatred waned. Or I got used to it."

"Why did you keep going back if you knew your relatives didn't like you?"

"My father made me. You see, he didn't want my mother traveling all that distance alone."

"Oh, yes, of course. I can see the wisdom in his decision."

Angie looked over at Veronica and Garrett. They were still talking ships, masts, and now Veronica was asking about pirates. Angie sighed, wondering if it was such a good idea to share her novels with her stepsister. It seemed she took them far too seriously. Looking back at Paden, Angie asked, "You didn't have to go on a ship during your army days?"

"No. I was in the cavalry."

"Union?"

"*Sí.* I was twenty-three when I enlisted," he said wistfully. "I was naive and ready to take on the world."

"Twenty-three? I was only twelve." She tipped her head, considering him. "That would make you. . .thirty-six now?"

"Your arithmetic is very good, Miz Huntington," he quipped.

She smirked. "Paden Montano, how did you ever live to be thirty-six years old without getting married?"

He shifted his position on the rock and his shoulder brushed up against hers. "Like my cousin, I never found the right woman," he answered plainly. He paused before adding, "And don't think I haven't looked. Over the past several years, I've courted a number of proper, Christian women. But none sparked my interest. . .until recently."

Even in the darkness, Angie picked up something meaningful in his tone, his gaze. In a flash, she knew what it was. "Are you interested in Veronica?" she whispered.

Paden leaned forward so their noses touched. "No."

"Oh." Chagrined, Angie brought her head back.

He chuckled.

"But there is someone in whom you are interested, is that correct?"

"*Sí,* I think there is."

"Here in San Francisco?" Angie watched Paden's head nod. "Do I know her?"

"You are too inquisitive for your own good." Paden crossed one booted foot over his knee and leaned back farther, his hand on the rock, just behind Angie.

"I'm only asking because if I know her, I could tell you if she's worth pursuing."

"Oh, I know she is worth pursuing. She is a very special young lady." He leaned against her, playfully bumping her shoulder with his. "And I do not need a matchmaker, so don't even consider it."

Angie inhaled sharply. "I would never do such a thing!"

"Yes, you would. You're a woman. I have four sisters, so I know how you females think."

Angie folded her arms, lifting a defiant chin. Beside her, she heard another of Paden's chuckles. She bristled. "All right, Mr. Know-it-all, if I guess this woman's name, will you tell me if I'm right?"

Paden took several seconds to mull over the question. Finally, he agreed.

Angie searched her mind for the name of every unattached female she knew. There weren't many in San Francisco—decent women, anyway. Many bachelors in need of wives took to ordering them through the mail.

"Thelma Bobkins," Angie said.

"Never heard of her."

"Hmm. . .you can't possibly be interested in Mrs. Carlisle. Her husband passed last year, but she has to be at least fifty."

"No, not Mrs. Carlisle—whoever she is."

Angie was about to make another calculated assumption when Garrett interrupted their little game. "I think we should start heading back," he said. "The wind is picking up. Angelique, you should have told me you were freezing, sitting there on that cold, hard boulder."

"On the contrary, I'm quite comfortable, thank you."

Upon hearing Paden's discreet, little snort of amusement, she realized the folly of her remark. Since they'd been sitting so close together, Garrett obviously presumed she was huddling beside his cousin for warmth.

Angie quickly stood. "But, you're right, I do think it's time to get back."

"Yes." Garrett looked between the two of them before offering Angie his arm.

Slipping her hand around his elbow, she glanced at Veronica, whose expression said nothing as to how she might view the situation. Angie decided to make it a point to ask later tonight, once their company departed.

The walk back seemed laden with tension. No one spoke, and Garrett kept up a lively pace, causing Angie to feel winded by the time they reached the house. On the front porch, he pulled her aside while Veronica and Paden went inside ahead of them.

"I must speak with you, Angelique."

"Tonight?"

"Yes. Right this minute."

Angie nibbled her lower lip indecisively. "Here? I'm freezing, remember?"

"Well, then, where? I have to talk to you. . .privately."

"How about tomorrow? No, it's Saturday and that will never do. Veronica and I have some orders to finish. How about Sunday after church?"

Garrett paused for a long moment, thinking it over.

"Surely whatever you have to discuss with me can wait until then," Angie added sweetly. "Can't it?"

His insistence dissolved before her very eyes. "Yes, I suppose you're right."

Angie smiled.

"We will both be in better frames of mind on Sunday, as you're shivering out here in the night air and I'm. . .well, I'm rather perturbed."

"Why is that?" She suspected the answer, but had to ask anyway.

To her dismay, he shrugged off her question. Then he surprised her further by whisking her into his muscled arms and kissing her soundly. Hard and possessively. When he released her, Angie stumbled backward. She touched her bruised mouth as tears gathered in her eyes. "How dare you treat me like that," she choked.

Garrett's reason quickly returned. "Angelique, I'm so sorry. . . ."

She barely heard the apology as she made for the door. She fumbled with the latch, but it soon opened and she ran into the house.

"Angelique, please—"

She ignored Garrett's calling her to come back and pushed past Veronica and Paden. Lifting her skirts, Angie took to the steps, two-by-two, and headed for her room. There she flounced onto her bed, sobbing. Why did men have to be so boorish? Why couldn't they be kind and tender. . .gentle?

Then suddenly one thing became very clear in Angie's mind. Captain Garrett Witherspoon was certainly not the man for her!

seven

"There, there, now," Veronica cooed, "don't cry."

Sitting on the edge of her bed, Angie dabbed her eyes with her hanky.

"You must admit, you and Mr. Montano did look quite cozy, sitting there on that rock. I can't really blame the captain for his jealous behavior."

"Veronica!" Angie gaped at her stepsister.

"Oh, now, I didn't say I condone it. I just. . .well, I understand, that's all."

"You're taking his side over mine."

"I'm doing no such thing," Veronica said. "It's just that after speaking with Captain Witherspoon tonight, I feel I know him better and he seems like an upstanding fellow; but then, of course, they all seem that way at first. Marriage must bring out the beast in men."

Angie ignored the remark. "What was the meaning of bringing up Silverstone tonight? You practically betrayed me in front of our guests. You, my most trusted friend. How could you do that to me?"

"Relax, my dear, I didn't set out to expose your past. I was merely testing Mr. Montano's integrity, that's all."

"And? Did he pass?" Angie couldn't keep the cynicism out of her voice.

"Yes, I suppose he did."

She cast Veronica a dubious look, and then several moments of silence passed between the two women. Angie played over in her mind the churlish way Garrett had kissed her good night.

Then suddenly beside her, Veronica started. Angie snapped out of her reverie. "Did you hear that?" Veronica asked in hushed tones.

"Hear what?"

"Upstairs. In the attic. It's him. I know it."

Angie inhaled deeply before letting out a slow breath. "Oh, not this again."

"Didn't you hear that thud?"

"No. And I've told you a million times, sister dear, that there aren't any ghosts up there. I haven't run into one yet."

Another bump, and this time Angie heard it, too. Veronica, however, nearly jumped out of her skin.

"It's the window," Angie said, recognizing the sound. "The breeze is out of the west tonight and likely blew it open. I'll run up and secure it."

"You are so brave."

Shaking her head at the foolishness, Angie grabbed the lighted lamp from the bedside table and headed for the stairs. A couple of years ago, she'd created her own sewing room up there, despite Veronica's superstitions and warnings. While Angie didn't believe in ghosts, per se, she believed Satan and his host were on their job twenty-four hours a day. Still, whenever Veronica's apprehensions began to affect her, Angie recalled the passage of Scripture that promised, "Greater is He that is in you than he that is in the world." No, Angie wasn't brave, but with the Holy Spirit's power, she had nothing to fear.

Reaching the dark attic now, she strode past a settee and several armchairs, each covered for protection with old linens. Beneath her, the floorboards creaked ominously, and she had to admit that by night this unfinished third story was, indeed, spooky. But, by day, Angie felt inspired by the breathtaking view of the ocean from her little sewing room at the front of the house. Entering her fabric-littered workplace, complete with dress forms, she saw that, as she'd suspected, the window had blown open. She shut and latched it tightly.

"Angelique?" Veronica's worry-riddled voice wafted up the stairway. "Are you all right, Dear?"

"I'm fine. It was the window we heard banging."

Lamp in hand, she made her way back downstairs. Veronica stood at the foot of the steps, waiting anxiously. For all her mettle, when it came to testing a man's integrity, Angie decided her stepsister was quite a goose concerning adventure novels and nighttime noises. There, Veronica's imagination excelled.

"Well, I think I'll turn in," Angie said. After a hug, she headed for her bedroom.

"Angelique?"

She paused, turning. "Yes?"

"I believe this is another of those times when having a man around might come in handy."

Angie had to grin. "Are you thinking of giving marriage another chance?"

"I. . .I don't know about that," Veronica stammered. "But I suppose we could board out the guestroom. Why most of the bachelors in San Francisco stay in boardinghouses. Perhaps Captain Witherspoon would—"

"Perish the thought! We're not set up for such an endeavor, and it wouldn't be proper to have him or any other gentleman living in this house in such close proximity to us—two unattached females."

"You're right, of course. I can't fathom why that notion went through my head."

I can, Angie mused as she padded the rest of the way to her room. Whenever she felt especially lonely, she meditated on the story of Adam and Eve in Genesis. God instituted marriage from the beginning. The Lord, Himself, performed the first wedding ceremony. It was right. It was good. God said so. And it was only natural for a woman to want to marry and raise children. Likewise, Angie deduced, a woman instinctively desired to be protected and cherished by the man she loved. Veronica was not immune to that innate yearning. Neither was Angie, and in her mind's eye she suddenly saw Garrett's serious eyes, strong chin, broad shoulders, and capable disposition. But as tempting as marriage to the captain seemed at this moment, Angie knew it wasn't God's will for her life. She sensed it now. Clearly.

But someday, she thought, crawling beneath the thick, down-filled comforter, someday the man of her dreams would walk into her life. He'd have a gentle hand, mild manner, a quiet voice, but unequivocal valor. He would accept her for who she'd been and who she'd become by God's grace. He'd love the Lord with all his heart, soul, and mind, and he'd love her so much, he'd die for her if he had to.

"Oh, for pity's sake," Angie murmured, rolling onto her side. "Now who's got the wild imagination?"

❧

The next day, Garrett stopped by the dress shop and asked to talk with Angie, but she had customers waiting to be fitted and couldn't get away. Veronica played mediator and the two of them seemed to have a beneficial conversation.

"He's ever so sorry," Veronica relayed at supper that evening.

"I believe he is, and all is forgiven." Angie paused to consider her stepsister for several long moments, before returning her attention to the seafood souffle that Tu Hing had prepared. "Your tone has changed. You no longer seem so opposed to Garrett. In fact, you seem rather for him. . .us."

"Well," she began, pressing back a stray lock of her honey-brown hair, "he strikes me as most sincere. One can't help feeling a bit sorry for the man. He is trying awfully hard to win your heart, you know."

"Yes," Angie agreed, "but unfortunately as time goes by, I feel less peace about marrying Garrett. And last night—" She sighed. "Last night I realized he's not the man for me."

"Surely a single kiss couldn't have frightened you that badly."

"No, not frightened exactly," she admitted, "but he manhandled me, don't you see? I promised myself when I left Silverstone that I would never again allow a man to take me or my affections by force, whether physically or emotionally."

"My dear, marriage cannot protect you from ever being in that situation again."

"Perhaps not," Angie said, thinking Veronica sounded more like her old self, "but God can. He'll protect me. . .and if it's His will that I should marry, He'll lead me to the right man someday." She grinned. "But for now I have my work—and after today, I have a lot of work!"

"And you have me," Veronica added. "Don't forget me."

❧

Sunday morning arrived and brought with it sunshine and a mild breeze. To Angie, it seemed a perfect day. She strolled to church with the Johnson family, who lived a few doors away. When they reached the small, brick house of worship near the Nob Hill area, Angie immediately saw Garrett's large frame folded into a pew about midway to the front. Beside him sat Paden. They seemed to chat amicably while Mrs. Matthison's fifteen-year-old daughter, Glenda, played the upright piano in the far left-hand corner of the sunlit sanctuary. Presently, she was plunking out "A Mighty Fortress Is Our God."

Angie slipped undetected into a pew across the aisle and two rows behind Garrett and Paden. Carla Chamberlain, a lovely new mother, was situated next to her and struck up a brief conversation about the weather and the diminishing Comstock Lode, but then Pastor Richards strode to the large, wooden pulpit. Smiling a greeting, the brown-eyed, copper-haired minister led them first in a few hymns before launching into his message.

"My dear friends," he began, "with the threat of economic depression looming over our city, we must remember what's really important in this life. . . ."

Angie listened intently, wondering what the monetary decline would mean for the Huntington House. She and Veronica had been hearing for some time that the decreased production of ore from the Comstock mine had significantly affected a number of San Francisco residents, but that wasn't anything new. With the rampant speculating of mining shares, many found themselves millionaires one day and paupers the next. Furthermore, the banks had seen their portion of fiscal peaks and valleys, too—so much so that Veronica felt leery of the financial institutions, but, at the same time, she acknowledged their importance in the community. Nevertheless, she insisted upon depositing only a fourth of their income from the dress shop, and the rest Veronica kept locked up tightly in a hidden safe at home.

Angie pushed aside her thoughts and forced herself to pay attention to the message.

"The Bible says one cannot serve God and money. You'll love the one and hate the other. Therefore we must lay up our treasures in Heaven." The reverend paused. "If Christ is our Joy, our Master, we can lose fortunes and still be happy."

Numerous voices in the sanctuary exclaimed, "Amen!" Angie inadvertently glanced across the aisle, only to find Garrett staring back at her. His hazel eyes seemed to beseech her. Obviously he felt badly about Friday night's miserable encounter. Angie returned an assuring smile, but then refocused on Pastor Richards, knowing the outcome of her meeting with Garrett later. If he proposed marriage, she'd have to decline. She didn't love him. She never would. *Lord,* she prayed, *I've trusted You with my soul. I trust You with my finances. . .certainly, I can trust You to bring me the right husband in Your perfect time.*

Pastor concluded his sermon and the congregation joined him in a hymn during the altar call. Several members went forward, and some even publicly announced that, regrettably, money had taken the Savior's place in their lives. The tearful smiles on their faces shone with divine forgiveness.

Once they were dismissed, Angie filed out of the pew. In the aisle, she met Garrett.

"I hope you still have time to speak with me, Angelique," he said in a formal, sophisticated tone, but his eyes were filled with anticipation.

"Why, yes, of course, Captain." Angie turned, and her gaze met Paden's. He nodded politely. She smiled a greeting. Looking back at Garrett, she said, "There's a small chamber in the rear of the church. Pastor Richards won't mind if we use it."

"Very good. Lead on."

She did, making her way through the throng of church-goers who were headed in the opposite direction.

"A bit like rowing against the tide," Garrett muttered near her ear as they inched forward. Finally, they reached the little room. The walls were unfinished and the air smelled musty. Angie took a seat on one of the long, wooden benches.

"I'll keep the door open for propriety's sake," Garrett said as he sat on the adjacent bench.

"Yes, please do."

A few moments of taut silence passed between them.

"I would like to start by begging your forgiveness, Angelique. I acted like a complete cad, taking such liberties with you Friday night."

"I have already forgiven you, Garrett," she said sincerely.

He smiled. "Thank you." He cleared his throat. "Now, as for the topic I wish to discuss with you. . . ."

Angie held her breath and sent up a quick prayer for wisdom.

"By now, you must know how I feel about you."

"Um, well, yes, I've gathered that you're quite fond of me."

Garrett grinned. "Fond, Angelique, cannot begin to describe my affections for you."

"I'm very flattered," she replied, looking down at her full skirt and picking at a piece of invisible lint.

He captured her hand in both of his, then sank to one knee. "Angelique, my sweet, I am in love with you. Say you'll marry me." He searched her face. "We'll sail off together, and once we're settled in Maine, I'll build you a home. Angelique," he whispered, "I will give up my career as a sea captain for you."

His words touched her heart in spite of her stiff resolve to turn him down. "Oh, Garrett, I—"

"Say yes."

Angie moistened her suddenly parched lips. "Garrett, I—"

"You're obviously speechless, my dear. A simple 'yes' will do."

"But—"

"Captain Witherspoon, sir?"

At the sound of the masculine voice coming from the doorway, Garrett swung his gaze around, and Angie looked up to find a young man standing there, his hat in hand. "Sir, I hate to disturb you. . . ."

Looking vexed, Garrett stood and brushed the dirt from his trousers. "What is it, Hopkins?"

"It's the *Jubilee*, Sir."

"What about her?"

"She's on fire."

"What? My ship's on fire?"

"Yes, Sir."

He turned to Angie with wide eyes. "Please excuse me."

"Of course."

Without another word, Garrett took off with the younger man running after him.

Angie sat back down, praying the fire would be extinguished soon and that Garrett's ship wouldn't suffer too much damage. Then she decided that refusing the dashing captain's marriage proposal wasn't going to be as easy as she imagined. He said he loved her. He'd give up his life on the sea for her. He'd make her a home. It was all she'd ever wanted to hear in a marriage proposal.

Couldn't I learn to love him, Lord? she asked her Heavenly Father. But the beat of her heart pounded out the answer: No, no, no, no, no, no, no.

Then suddenly a long shadow appeared on the dusty, plank floor in front of her. Glancing at the doorway, she saw Paden leisurely reclining against the wooden frame. He held his wide-brimmed hat in his hands and he wore a dark gray shirt, ebony vest, and jacket. His charcoal-colored trousers were neatly stuffed into shiny, black boots.

"Well?"

"Well, what?" Angie rose from the bench.

"Did my cousin propose as we suspected?"

"Yes. Unfortunately, his ship caught fire before I could give him my answer."

Paden shook his dark head. "Such a pity about his ship. I was the one who told Garry's first mate, Luther Hopkins, where to find him. I hope the vessel is not completely destroyed."

"Yes, I hope not."

Paden pushed himself off the doorjamb and stepped forward. "You look. . .worried, *mi amada*. What's wrong?" He stopped just inches away and stroked Angie's cheek with the knuckle of his forefinger.

"I'm just. . .thinking," she replied softly, unnerved by his touch and wondering why.

"Thinking of marrying my cousin after all?"

"Yes. I mean, no." She shook her head, feeling oddly flustered. Sidestepping Paden, she paused by the doorway. "What I meant is, I reconsidered briefly, but I really cannot accept. That's my final answer."

When no reply was forthcoming, Angie peeked over her shoulder at Paden. He grinned back at her. "Miz Huntington," he began on a formal note, "may I escort you home?"

Angie turned the rest of the way around, her skirts swirling at her ankles. She thought over his offer, his touch, his romantic Spanish endearments and narrowed her gaze suspiciously. "Paden Montano, are you flirting with me?"

"*Sí, señorita*. How could you tell?"

"Lucky guess," she quipped.

Smiling, Paden offered his arm. Angie threaded her hand around his elbow. They made their way back through the sanctuary and, walking up the aisle beside him, Angie experienced a strange stirring in her heart. Would she ever be a bride, stepping elegantly down the aisle, heading for the altar and not the front doors?

Lord, she prayed for the second time that morning, *I've trusted You with my soul. I trust You with my finances. . .certainly, I can trust You to bring me the right husband in Your perfect time.*

eight

Outside, the sun shone brightly from its noonday perch in a blue, cloudless sky. Angie inhaled the fresh, sea air, but then noticed Paden's troubled expression. Following his gaze, she saw thick, black smoke towering into the air.

"I think the fire at the harbor is worse than we first suspected," he murmured. "And from the looks of it, I'd wager that Garrett's ship is not the only one involved."

Angie inhaled sharply, praying this fire wouldn't consume the city like the one back in '51. She'd heard horror stories about that day.

Paden turned to face her. "I'm sorry, but I need to go and see if I can help."

"I'm coming with you."

He looked as though he might argue the point, but then a hint of a grin caused his sleek, black mustache to twitch. "As you wish."

Taking her hand, he hurried to the corner, where he summoned a hackney. After they climbed in, Angie had several minutes to catch her breath before they reached the harbor. When the carriage pulled to a halt, Paden helped her down before giving the Chinese driver his fare. Next, he took hold of Angie's elbow and propelled her toward the chaotic scene.

Firemen shouted orders to each other while they manned the steam engines and hoses, aiming for the three smoldering vessels. The police kept spectators at a safe distance. Sailors ran up and down gangplanks, unloading precious commodities before the flames consumed them.

"There's Garry," Paden said, pointing off to the left. Then, with his hand beneath her elbow, he guided her forward, through the busy throng.

Garrett frowned, watching their approach. "What possessed you to bring Angelique down here? This is no place for a lady."

Angie glanced at Paden. "She insisted," he stated simply.

"Well, you could have refused to bring her," Garrett muttered before turning to Angie. "My dear, the docks are no place for a woman."

"But I wanted to help. Paden said he was coming, so I. . .I *forced* him to bring me along."

"You forced him, eh?" Lifting a brow, Garrett gave his cousin a doubtful look before bringing his gaze back to Angie. "That's kind of you, my sweet, but now the fire is out on the *Jubilee*. There's nothing more any of us can do at the moment. As you can see, there's extensive damage, but she's still afloat. I guess that's something to be thankful for."

Angie had never seen Garrett's ship before, and she guessed it had once been a fine-looking vessel. Now her masts were blackened and burned, although the bow seemed to have suffered the most damage.

"Doesn't look like we'll make it to Maine before Thanksgiving, Angelique," Garrett said, gazing at his clipper. "Not on the *Jubilee,* anyway."

She frowned at him, then looked at Paden, who gave her a curious glance.

"And she might not be worth rebuilding at this point," Garrett continued somewhat pensively before returning his attention to Angie. "But at least I have you. This loss is much easier to accept, knowing our future together awaits. And what's stopping us from seeking passage on another ship?"

Before Angie could reply, Paden cleared his throat loudly. "Is there something you haven't told me, Garry?"

"Why, yes, I guess there is." Lifting her hand and gazing into her eyes, he said, "I asked Angelique to marry me after church today, and she accepted."

"She did? Why, Miz Huntington," Paden drawled, "I'm surprised that you didn't tell me the good news, yourself. Congratulations."

"But I—"

"I think she's a bit overwhelmed," Garrett cut in, slipping his arm around Angie's waist. "In fact, I really ought to take her home. I'm sure this fire has upset her greatly."

"By all means," Paden replied.

"I am perfectly fine," Angie protested. She gave Paden a pointed stare, hoping he'd help her out of this most awkward position, but he merely glared at her, his expression unreadable.

Then before another word could be uttered, Garrett escorted her down the dock and away from the waterfront. He managed to hire a coach and assisted Angie inside. "I'm afraid I smell like a chimney," he said apologetically after he'd seated himself beside her.

"Garrett, there's been a terrible misunderstanding."

"With regard to my cousin? Oh, don't worry about him. I suspect he's been trifling with you, but that will change now that we're betrothed."

"But that's where the misunderstanding lies, Garrett. We're not betrothed. I never accepted your marriage proposal. I never had a chance."

"You didn't? I'm sure I heard you agree to become my wife."

"No," Angie replied, shaking her head, "you didn't hear that because I never said it."

"Well, say it now, my sweet."

"I can't," she said softly, ruefully. Her past flashed across her memory like a searing reminder not to even be tempted by this matrimonial offer. "Garrett, I can't marry you. I'm sorry."

His expression fell, and Angie felt terrible for hurting him.

"I'm sorry," she stated again. "But I know it's not right. It's not God's will. I've prayed about it."

"And so have I!"

"Yes, but were you listening for an answer or were you telling the Lord your intentions?"

Garrett brought his chin back indignantly.

"I do that sometimes," Angie confessed. "I tell the Lord those things I wish to accomplish and ask Him to bless them, never thinking to ask if my plans are in accordance with His will for my life."

"I am sure I have not misunderstood my God," Garrett replied tersely.

Angie didn't reply. It seemed senseless to argue the point. A few moments of taut silence passed and then the carriage came to a stop. "Thank you for seeing me home."

Garrett took her hand. "Angelique, please—"

She pulled out of his grasp. "I'm so sorry. The last thing on earth I want to do is hurt you, but I can't marry you."

His features hardened. "Very well, Miss Huntington," he said in stiff formality. Then he climbed out of the hack and helped her down.

As soon as her feet touched the ground, Angie fled to the front door with tears of remorse stinging her eyes.

❧

Paden lurked in the darkness outside an impressive gentlemen's club. Hours ago, he'd seen Harry Munson enter with William Rosewahl, a bank president, and Hiram Littleton, a medical doctor. Both men were in the upper echelon of San Francisco's society. Andy's theory had been correct.

Paden recalled his first day in this city. He had walked into the police station and announced himself as an old friend of the police chief. That hadn't been a lie, either. He and Andy Stephenson had fought in the cavalry together, so when Paden informed him that he was employed as a Pinkerton agent and stated his business, Andy told him about the corruption going on among many of the city's affluent citizens.

So that explains why I couldn't find Munson among the gambling dens and saloons, Paden mused. The money Munson stole during the train robbery in Missouri had earned him a place with some of San Francisco's elite. Unfortunately, Paden couldn't get into the club to apprehend the renegade since it was a "members only" establishment. Obviously, Rosewahl and Littleton had sponsored Munson as their guest.

He waited, poised and ready, praying for protection. Paden knew he had to nab Munson soon. The longer the man went unchecked, the easier it would become for him to discover Paden's identity as a Pinkerton agent.

Just then, the doors to the gentlemen's club opened and out stepped two obviously intoxicated males, singing off-key at the top of their lungs. "Way down upon the Swanee River, far, far away, there's where my heart is turnin' ever, there's where the old folks stay. . . ."

Paden rolled his eyes and shook his head. The door to the club opened once more, and another man exited. It was Harry Munson.

Drawing his gun, Paden watched from the shadows as Munson headed in his direction, right behind the two drunks who continued to sing, "All the world is sad and dreary, everywhere I roam; Oh, brother, how my heart grows weary, far from the old folks at home."

As the group of three men neared, Paden suddenly recognized Garrett as one of the off-key vocalists.

Paden stood there, stunned. Garry? Drunk? How was that possible? However, in that moment of distraction, Munson turned the corner. Stepping out from the darkened alley, Paden followed him. . .until his cousin's voice halted him in his tracks.

"Well, if it isn't my favorite relative," he slurred.

Paden stopped and pivoted. The other drunken man had climbed into a carriage that swiftly went on its way down the street.

"You are a disgrace, Garry. Look at you," Paden said, disgusted. "You are a Christian man. You have no business getting drunk."

"I couldn't help it," he replied, slurring his words. "First the *Jubilee* and then Angelique. A man can only take so much. . . ."

"Come on. I will take you back to the boardinghouse."

"No, no, I can't go there. Mrs. Crabtree doesn't like to rent to men who indulge in spirited beverages, and I promised her I was not of that inclination. I wasn't, either. . .until tonight." Garrett grinned and swayed slightly.

"Then you will have to come to the hotel with me."

"I am forever indebted to your kindness," Garrett mumbled, tripping over every syllable.

Paden sighed and led him down the street to a waiting hack. "Take us to the Oriental Hotel."

The driver nodded.

Paden helped his brawny cousin into the coach and then sat opposite from him. "What happened with Angelique?"

"She turned me down," Garrett lamented. "She said she can't marry me."

The words echoed in Paden's mind. *She turned him down.* He couldn't help but feel elated at the news. Except, he shouldn't; his cousin was hurting badly. Then he realized that if he won Angie's heart, it would be a bittersweet victory.

Garrett narrowed his gaze. "It's your fault she turned me down."

"Mine?"

"Yes, yours. You. . .you charmed her, knowing she was the love of my life. You. . .you're nothin' but a philanderer."

Paden grinned. He'd been called worse. "And you, *Primo,*

are very drunk. But you'll think clearer in the morning—after your headache subsides."

❧

Sunshine streamed through the open draperies of the hotel room, shining in Garrett's eyes. He moaned and Paden chuckled before swallowing the last of his coffee. He'd purchased a pot full of the steaming brew in the downstairs dining room and now poured himself a second cup.

"You had better wake up, or I'll drink all the coffee myself."

In reply, Garrett moaned again. "I'm sure thugs beat me to a pulp last night."

Paden chuckled again. "No, I'm afraid you were your own worst enemy."

"Apparently. I can't imagine what I was thinking. I have never been drunk in my life. I have never even touched liquor. . .before last night."

"I hope you will never touch it again."

Garrett squinted at him, looking as if it hurt to do so. "On my honor, I never will. The morning after is horrible!" He fell back on the pillows and groaned.

Smiling, Paden sipped his coffee. "Any news on what started the fire yesterday?"

"It was arson. Authorities have incarcerated the fellow—a disgruntled sailor who lost his job and decided to burn down the harbor."

"Hmm. . . ."

"I can't help but wonder why God allowed the *Jubilee* to be one of the vessels that burned. Why didn't the Lord protect it? He knows shipping is my occupation, my livelihood. Now that Angelique. . .well, it hardly serves my purposes to retire from my life on the sea."

Paden thought it over. "I'm afraid I don't have any answers for you."

"No, no one does. This is between my God and me."

"Perhaps so, but I do have a confession to make."

"Oh?"

"*Sí.*" Paden knew it had to be said. "I would like nothing better than to win Angie for myself."

"I figured." Garrett propped himself up on one elbow and strained to look at him through the bright sunshine. "Angie, is it?"

Paden shrugged.

"Well, I'll tell you one thing, she's a lady and she's not about to marry a gunfighter."

"True enough. That's why I have been thinking along the lines of buying land in Texas and settling down."

"You? Settle down?" Garrett laughed and collapsed against the pillows again. "Now that's funny."

"It is not half as amusing as you giving up your life on the sea," Paden returned.

"Touché," Garrett quipped. He was silent for several long moments. "I guess love has a way of warping a man's thinking."

"I guess it does."

"But you can't possibly be in love with Angelique. You hardly know her. You only recently met. You've seen her, what. . .twice?"

"And what do you know of her?"

"I know she's shy, sweet, in need of a man's protection."

Paden smirked, thinking about Angie down by the wharf, witnessing to the working girls.

"She's a Christian."

"Have you heard her salvation testimony?"

"Well, no. . .have you?"

"*Sí.*"

Garrett bolted upright, then winced. "You have?"

Paden nodded. "And what about her family background," he began carefully. "What do you know of it?"

"She's a Huntington, a distant relative of Mrs. Veronica

Huntington, whose husband was killed at Vicksburg. He died a hero's death. The Huntington family is respected in San Francisco."

Paden pursed his lips thoughtfully. "Does Angie have sisters? Brothers?"

Garrett looked momentarily uncomfortable. "Not sure. Do you know?"

"If I recall, she only has one stepsister."

Garrett gave him an underhanded look.

"And you, of course, know the color of her eyes."

"Of course. They're. . .um, green, I think."

"They are dark blue, like the sky just as the stars begin to shine."

"You are so poetic," Garrett stated facetiously. "That's why the women adore you." He threw off the bedcovers and stood. "I knew Angelique's eyes were blue. I've seen 'em a hundred times. I just couldn't remember."

"Understandable."

"Tell you what, Paden. You go ahead and try to win Angelique's heart with your flowery words and Latin charm. She turned me down, so I guess that means she's fair game. But I'm not giving up that easily, and I will continue to pursue her. . .since it looks like I'm stuck in San Francisco for awhile anyway. Your job, whatever it is, will be taking you away soon, and then Angelique will forget all about the smooth-talking gunslinger who broke her heart. She'll realize that I'm the best man for her."

Paden thought it over, then shook his head. "No, I don't want a war over a woman to come between us, Garry. There has to be another way to settle this matter. We're family. We're blood."

He snorted derisively as he poured himself a cup of coffee. "Relatives or not, the war has begun."

nine

Fog had rolled in off the Pacific as Angie made her way to the bank Monday afternoon. Because of the overcast sky, everything around her looked dismal. It matched her mood. She knew she'd done the right thing in turning down Garrett's proposal yesterday, yet she felt so disappointed. What if she never got another offer of marriage?

Veronica said she was better off "unattached." Perhaps she was right. A husband seemed like an awful lot of trouble.

Arriving at the bank, Angie pulled open the door and let herself inside. She walked to the window and made her transaction. When she turned to leave, Mr. Rosewahl stepped into her path. "Miss Huntington, how nice to see you today."

She smiled. "Why, thank you."

"The dress shop business is booming, I hope."

"We keep busy, yes." Angie was careful as to how she replied since Veronica refused to put all their income into the savings account. Mr. Rosewahl wouldn't be pleased to hear it, and he'd likely give the two of them a lengthy speech on the proper safekeeping of their funds.

"Glad to hear it," the man replied, staring down his beak-like nose at her. "And where is your Mexican friend today?"

"Excuse me?"

"That man you were with on Friday. . .what was his name? Montano?"

"Oh, yes."

"My wife thinks perhaps there are wedding bells in your future. She has this way of stargazing, you know."

Angie gave the man a polite smile. She'd told him before

that she was a Christian and didn't believe in fortunetellers. Besides, Mrs. Rosewahl was forever saying that wedding bells were in her future.

"Mr. Montano might be the right one," the banker continued. "What does he do for a living?"

"Um. . ." While Angie had promised to keep Paden's secret, she knew she couldn't lie. "I believe he works closely with the United States government," she said diplomatically.

"Oh, really? How very interesting. Do you think he makes a good living?"

"I'm sure he does."

"Well, a woman has to be certain of these things before entering into marriage, Miss Huntington."

"Thank you for your concern, but I don't believe I'll be marrying Paden or anyone else very soon."

"But it's written in the stars, Miss Huntington. Now, about Mr. Montano. . .where is he from?"

"He was born in the United States and reared in Mexico."

"Ah, of course. Mexico."

Angie stepped toward the door. "Good day to you, Mr. Rosewahl."

"One more question, please. I hope you don't mind. I don't mean to be intrusive, I'm just. . .well, as you said, *concerned*."

She nodded, but suddenly something about this whole conversation made her very nervous.

"Is your Mr. Montano the same one who was a sheriff in the Arizona Territory? Silverstone, Arizona?"

Angie felt herself grow pale, sensing that Mr. Rosewahl had done some investigation work. She momentarily debated how to answer him. Then she decided honesty was the best recourse. "Yes, as a matter of fact, Paden was sheriff in Silverstone."

Rosewahl's eyes narrowed. "He's a renowned gunman,

Miss Huntington. How could you possibly be acquainted with a gunman?"

She sighed, hoping she seemed nonchalant. "As I mentioned, he's Captain Garrett Witherspoon's cousin."

"Ah, yes, that's right. The captain. A pity about the fire at the docks yesterday. I hope his ship is unharmed. Any marital prospects there?"

"No, I'm afraid not. Now, I really must get back to the shop."

"Of course. Good day, Miss Huntington. I'm sorry to have detained you."

Angie left the bank, but as she strolled down the boardwalk, a dark foreboding crept up her spine. Of course, it wasn't a secret that Paden had been sheriff in Silverstone. That tidbit couldn't have been difficult to discover. Still, the fact that Mr. Rosewahl had found it out at all caused alarm bells to jangle in the depth of her being.

She increased her pace, then darted across the street and walked up the block to the Oriental Hotel. Reaching the four-story building, she entered the lobby and nearly collided with Garrett, who was on his way out.

"Angelique! I mean. . .Miss Huntington."

She inhaled sharply. "Good afternoon. . .Captain." She glanced over his attire and thought he looked a bit rumpled. Perhaps many of his belongings had been lost in the fire. Regardless, his thick, brown hair was neatly parted and combed. He looked clean-shaven and he smelled of masculine woodsy-spicy soap. Where had she smelled that fragrance before?

"The fog rolled in quickly, didn't it?" Garrett remarked, looking up at the sky.

"Yes, it did."

He nodded before glancing over his shoulder. "Do you have business here at the hotel?"

"Yes, I need to speak with Paden. Is he in?" Garrett's

expression fell, and so as not to give him the wrong impression, Angie quickly added, "It's an official matter."

"I see. Well, I'm sorry to say that my cousin is not in his hotel room. I just came from there."

"Oh. You're looking for him, too?"

"Not really. It's a long story—one you would not be interested in hearing, I'm sure."

"I'll take your word for it." Angie gave him a little smile.

"You can leave a message for Paden at the desk if you wish."

She shook her head. "No need. It's not pressing. It can wait."

A soft light entered Garrett's hazel eyes and, once more, Angie noted how very handsome he was. Perhaps before rejecting his marriage proposal, she should have discussed the matter with Pastor Richards.

No, no. . .she'd made the right choice. Why was she second-guessing herself?

"May I escort you somewhere?"

"I suppose I'll just return to the shop."

"Well, how about that!" He grinned. "I'm heading in the same direction."

Angie smiled in skeptical acquiescence. Why was Garrett being so nice to her? She'd rejected him yesterday. She would have expected him to be cold and indifferent.

He offered his arm, and Angie looped her hand around his elbow. She sighed inwardly as they began to walk. She would just have to think of some other way to tell Paden about Mr. Rosewahl.

❧

As it happened, Veronica invited Garrett to dinner. He readily accepted and Angie was surprised that the evening passed as pleasantly as it did. Garrett refrained from giving her long, amorous looks which, in turn, made Angie feel more comfortable in his presence. They talked and laughed and enjoyed each other's company.

"He's really a very nice man," Veronica said once Garrett left.

Angie began climbing the stairs to her bedroom. "Does that surprise you, sister dear?"

Just behind her, Veronica produced a light, little flutter of a laugh. "As a matter of fact, it does."

Grinning, Angie gave her a quick, parting hug in the hallway. "Good night."

"Sweet dreams, Darling," she returned in a motherly tone.

In her room, Angie changed into her night clothes and brushed out her long hair. She felt bone tired from not having slept well the night before and yet she felt completely at peace, satisfied, and contented. In retrospect, Angie realized that she'd felt awful for hurting Garrett yesterday, but seeing as he'd taken the news so favorably, she was no longer riddled with guilt.

She crawled into bed and under the thick patchwork quilt that Veronica had painstakingly brought from back East. Closing her eyes, she said her prayers. *Thank You, Lord, for keeping me safe today. Thank You for blessing our business and putting food on our table, clothes on our backs. Thank You for Veronica and I pray for her soul, Lord. Please continue to work in her heart. Help me to be a good witness to her, a testimony of Your love. . . .*

On that thought, Angie drifted off to sleep. However, in no time, it seemed, she was awakened by an odd-sounding noise. She sat up in bed, straining to hear in the darkness, and the strangest sensation stole over her being. She sensed another's presence. Could there really be someone in her bedroom?

Fear paralyzed her for a long moment, but soon her wits returned. Then, just as she moved to get out of bed to investigate, a leather-encased hand clapped over her mouth. Angie's arms flailed as she fought her assailant, but he quickly overpowered her.

"Hush, *mi amada,*" came the soft, familiar voice with its subtle accent. "It is I."

Angie relaxed slightly, her breath coming and going in quick spurts, while questions darted through her mind. Paden slowly lifted his gloved hand from her mouth and moved away. "What are you doing here?" she hissed at him. "You scared me half to death!"

A pause.

"Paden?" Angie's ire was rising quickly, but his next words cut to the quick.

"I've been shot. I am wounded. I need your help."

ten

"You're hurt?"

"*Sí,*" Paden replied.

"Where? Is it bad? Why didn't you go to the hospital?"

"Shh, Angie, keep your voice down. No one must know that I am here. It's a long story, and I will explain, but first. . . please, if you could look at the gunshot wound. It's in my right arm. . .and my chest, I think."

Angie pulled on her robe, tying it at the waist. "You think? What do you mean, you 'think'?"

Paden just sighed, obviously in pain.

Assessing the situation, Angie decided the best place to tend to Paden was in her sewing room. Hurriedly, she ushered him up the stairs.

"How did you get into my bedroom?" she had to ask.

"I climbed onto the verandah, then in through the window."

Angie lit a lamp, feeling amazed. "You climbed to the second-story verandah with an injured arm?"

"It is incredible what a man can do when his blood is racing. . .and God's angels are guiding his every move."

"Yes, I suppose it is, although I don't approve of such behavior as climbing into a woman's bedroom in the middle of the night."

"*Sí,* I understand, and I would not have done it except for my desperate situation."

Somewhat appeased, Angie helped him take off his jacket, vest, and shirt, then evaluated his injuries.

"God was certainly protecting you," she said. "The bullet went clear through your arm, missing the bone. You were only grazed on the right side of your chest—except you've got a good-sized gash there."

She led him across the room and helped him onto the fainting couch. He closed his eyes in obvious relief. However, Angie thought he'd lost a fair amount of blood, judging from his stained clothing and pallid complexion. She knelt beside him. "You need a doctor, Paden. Your wounds need to be properly cleaned, and the one in your arm needs stitching."

"You are a competent nurse, Angie," he replied without opening his eyes. "I know you have patched up gunshot wounds before."

"Sure," she remarked with a trace of cynicism, "except the last unfortunate soul who I attended died on me."

"I promise I will not die."

After a dubious look, Angie took hold of some scrap material and bound the wound on his arm to stop the bleeding. "Why can't I fetch the doctor?"

"Because I cannot trust anyone right now. Harry Munson, the outlaw I was hired to find, got away, and now he knows I'm after him. One of San Francisco's prominent doctors—a man named Littleton—was killed tonight, and a banker named Rosewahl was injured or may be dead."

Angie gasped. "Mr. Rosewahl?"

"*Sí,* I shot both men. I had no choice. It was an ambush, and I walked right into it. Munson drew on me first, but fortunately, his aim is not so good. Then Littleton and Rosewahl pulled out pistols, and. . .well, I had no other choice than to defend myself. I don't think there were witnesses, but I'm sure there are people in high places who would like nothing better than to slap me with a murder charge."

"Oh, Paden!" Angie felt afraid for him.

"Tomorrow, I will have to get a message to the chief of police. He is a friend of mine."

Angie nodded, realizing his dire predicament. "I'll help you."

"*Gracias*."

"Oh, Paden, I hope I didn't aid the ambush."

"What do you mean?" he asked weakly.

"When I went to the bank this afternoon, Mr. Rosewahl asked me a host of questions about you. He knew you'd been the sheriff in Silverstone."

"What did you tell him?"

"Nothing he didn't already know. And I went to the Oriental Hotel looking for you, to inform you about the incident, but I ran into Garrett and he said you weren't there."

Paden let out a long, slow breath. "He lied to you. I was in my hotel room all afternoon."

"He lied?"

"*Sí*. He is determined to win your heart even though you turned him down once. He will not take no for an answer."

"Of all the despicable things!"

"Angie?" Paden's voice was but a whisper. "Could you sew me up before I bleed to death?"

"You're not going to bleed to death," she retorted. "No such luck."

His sleek, black mustache twitched as he grinned. Angie quickly made her way downstairs to fetch some supplies. When she arrived back at her sewing room, she coaxed Paden into taking a healthy dose of the laudanum she used to cure her sick headaches.

"You don't want to feel this, Paden. Trust me."

"*Sí,* I trust you."

His words had an odd effect on her heart. She felt flattered. Privileged. Paden Montano didn't trust just anyone.

Carefully, Angie began to clean his bloody wounds with hot, soapy water. By the time she'd finished, Paden was sound asleep, his chest rising and falling in deep, even rhythm. She prayed before she began to stitch the hole in his right arm. Piercing another human being with a needle made her queasy, but Paden was right: She'd done it before. Sometimes at gunpoint.

At Chicago Joe's house of ill-fame, Angie had been known for being handy with a needle, whether it came to sewing a hem or torn flesh. Gunfights were not uncommon among the desperados who frequented the establishment, and Paden, the town's only lawman, had his hands full. Most times, however, he let the riffraff shoot it out, figuring it saved him some work. Angie had always thought he was a fair man. Fair, but hardened. She supposed he had to be.

The night he and Pastor Luke came to rescue her had completely caught her unawares. She could still recall the way her heart had lurched at the sight of Paden stepping through the door of her dark, dingy room at the brothel. She'd respected him until that moment. However, he soon commanded her to pack her bags and informed her she was going out the window and into the waiting wagon in the alley below. Angie's head had spun with incredulity.

And now here he was, back in her life.

And now here she was, patching up another gunfighter.

Oh, Lord, when will it ever end?

Angie knotted off the end of the thread, deciding she'd done as good a job as any doctor. She wrapped a clean piece of material around Paden's upper arm. It would be a sufficient bandage. Rising, she stretched out the kink in her back and searched the attic for a blanket. She found one and covered Paden. Then, lamp in hand, she retired to her bedroom, making sure there were no telltale bloodstains on the floor for Veronica to find in the morning.

❧

When the first pinks of dawn lighted the eastern sky, Angie forced her weary body out of bed. Donning her robe, she hurried downstairs before Veronica awoke and before Tu Hing began his day by preparing breakfast. Finding the kitchen empty, Angie made a meal for Paden. Later, she would smuggle up some hot coffee. For now, this would have to do.

Reaching the attic, she set down the wooden tray she'd been carrying and examined her patient.

Paden cracked open one eye. "Have I died and gone to heaven? I see an angel."

Angie smirked. "Save your charm for some other poor, unsuspecting woman. It won't work on me."

"No? Such a pity."

"For whom?"

Fully awake now, Paden struggled to a sitting position. "Such sparring first thing in the morning is not healthy for a man."

"Neither are gunfights," Angie quipped. "Here, I brought you some breakfast."

Paden looked at the tray holding a plate of roasted chicken, rice, a chunk of bread, and half a jar of fresh milk. Then he inspected his arm and flexed his hand. Next, he tried to bend his arm at the elbow, but moaned in agony.

"I hope you didn't just burst all my stitches," Angie said, frowning at him. "That wound is going to take awhile to heal."

"*Sí*, I know. But I had to try it out."

Shaking her head at him, she pivoted. "I need to get dressed, but I'll try to bring you some coffee before I leave for the shop."

Paden caught her hand as she tried to leave. "Thank you, Angie," he whispered.

"You're welcome," she replied, feeling oddly unsettled.

He released her, and she continued on her way downstairs. Once inside her bedroom, she wondered why she had suddenly felt so flustered. Was Paden's gratitude so hard to accept? Or was it the way he'd looked right through her with those deep brown eyes of his?

Angie pushed her thoughts of Paden aside and pulled a dark gray skirt and white blouse from the polished oak wardrobe. After she'd dressed, she brushed back her hair, pinning it in a bun and adorning it with a silvery ribbon.

"Good morning, Angelique," Veronica said, meeting her in the hallway. "Did you sleep well?"

She stifled a yawn. "Actually, not. I hope you slept better than I did."

"I did, thank you." Veronica's greenish-brown eyes seemed to sparkle. "I had a lovely time last night. Would you like to know a secret?"

Angie smiled.

"I dreamt about Captain Witherspoon! I was Cinderella and he was Prince Charming. We were at a ball given by the Hathaways."

Angie couldn't help the little giggle that slipped through her lips.

"He asked me to dance, and I accepted. We waltzed all night long. . .and then I woke up."

"And you're not tired? After waltzing all night long?"

Veronica cast her glance from beneath lowered lashes. "It was a dream, Angelique. Nothing more than a silly old dream."

They sat down at their places in the dining room, and Tu Hing brought their tea. He greeted each lady with a polite smile before returning to the kitchen.

"You know, sister dear," Angie said, deciding to forget Garrett's lie from yesterday—at least for the time being, until she could confront him about it, "I always thought you and the good captain would make a handsome pair."

"Bite your tongue. It'll take a miracle for me to marry him or any other man."

Angie grinned and sipped her tea. Little did Veronica know that God was in the miracle business!

eleven

Angie managed to sneak some coffee up to the attic sewing room for Paden. Mr. Hing had seemed curious as to her request, since she wasn't a coffee drinker. Despite the questions so obviously swirling around in his head, he didn't speak his mind, for which Angie was grateful.

"*Gracias*, Angie."

"You're welcome," she replied, setting down the hot, steaming brew. "I also brought the newspaper and a Bible for you." She watched Paden flex his hand. "I hope you're planning to take it easy today."

"*Sí,* I don't have much choice." He met her gaze. "Therefore, I need another favor."

Angie folded her arms and lifted her chin, preparing herself. "Yes?"

"Could you take a message to the chief of police for me? His name is Andy Stephenson."

"I know what his name is. Doesn't everyone in San Francisco?"

Paden shrugged.

"What would you like me to tell him?"

He grinned. "Thank you, Angie. I am indebted to you."

She shook her head, unable to help the smile. "You saved my life, Paden. This is the least I can do for you. Now what's the message?"

"Tell Andy that I am alive, but wounded. Tell him I am the one who killed Littleton, and possibly Rosewahl. Please explain to him that it was self-defense. Then ask him to wire the Pinkerton office for me."

Angie nodded. "All right."

"Also let Andy know that I am willing to turn myself in if necessary. For now, it is best that I stay in hiding. I cannot defend myself, should I meet up with a desperado who wants to settle an old score."

Angie immediately felt concerned. "Is that likely?"

Paden shrugged. "It is always a possibility."

She frowned, thinking it must be an awful existence for Paden to have to constantly watch his back and be ready to draw. It was a lifestyle of which she wanted no part. Gunfighters and desperados. . .she'd had her fill of them.

"Well, I'd best get myself to the dress shop. Veronica is waiting for me."

"*Sí,* then you had better go. But one last question, *por favor*. Do I need to worry that your hired man or anyone else may come up here?"

"No. Veronica believes this attic is haunted by the ghost of her late husband and she's convinced poor Mr. Hing of it." Angie smiled. "No one will bother you up here."

"Except, perhaps, the ghost of Mr. Huntington."

"Why, Paden Montano, I would have never guessed you to be fooled by silly superstitions."

His wry grin told her that he was only teasing.

She smiled again and stepped toward the stairwell. "I usually have errands in the afternoon, so that's when I'll go to the police department. I'll try to get back here to sneak up some lunch for you."

"Don't worry about me, Angie. I will be fine."

"You'll rest?"

Paden grinned sheepishly. "I will rest."

Appeased, Angie made her way down two flights of stairs, grabbed her shawl by the front entrance, then left the house for the shop just a few blocks away.

It wasn't until midafternoon when Angie found time to

leave the shop. At the bank, the clerk informed her that Mr. Rosewahl was at the hospital in grave condition. She lent a sympathetic ear, but said nothing about her knowledge of the incident. Then it was on to the police station. In discovering San Francisco's history, she'd learned that organized law enforcement had begun more than twenty years ago. Now however, there were rumors flitting about with regard to corruption among some of the officers. Veronica, especially, relished any gossip pertaining to innocent citizens who were incarcerated for crimes they never committed. Then, while they attempted to prove their guiltlessness, the renegade police raided the prisoners' homes, thieving and looting as they went. Angie was sure the stories were highly exaggerated because she'd never known anyone who had personally experienced such a thing. Nevertheless, she approached the uniformed gentleman at the front desk with caution.

"May I help you, Ma'am?"

"Yes. I'd like to speak with Chief Stephenson, please."

The young man shook his dark brown head. "Sorry, Ma'am. He's awfully busy today." He grinned charmingly. "Perhaps I can help."

"No, I'm afraid I need to speak with the chief."

"What about?"

"A personal matter."

"I see." The officer scratched his head and glanced over his shoulder and down a long hallway. "Well, like I said, he's awfully busy."

"I'm a friend."

The officer's brows shot up. "Oh?"

"Well, a friend of a friend, I guess you might say."

"A friend of a friend, eh? That sounds kind of suspicious to me."

Angie felt herself growing frustrated and nervous. She hadn't expected to be interrogated.

"What's your name, Ma'am?"

She nibbled her lower lip. Ought she give it to him? What if he were in on the corruption and made trouble for her and Veronica? Angie had the welfare of the dress shop to think about.

"All right, then, Ma'am. What's your friend's name?"

Once more, she hesitated. Would Paden mind if she gave his name or did he say he'd already given it. He'd seen his friend, the chief. Surely he'd been questioned, too.

"Now, look, Ma'am, I can't let just anyone see Mr. Stephenson. If you're *somebody*, perhaps—"

"Mrs. Paden Montano," Angie blurted without giving the matter a second thought. "Please tell the chief Mrs. Paden Montano is here to see him."

The officer gave her a once-over with a narrowed brown-eyed gaze, then looked increasingly suspicious.

"Just tell the chief I'm here to see him, all right?" Her patience was waning.

"Sure. . .Mrs. Montano."

Looking wary, the man left his perch and walked down the hallway, knocking on a door near the far end. Angie heard muffled voices and then another man joined the first officer and they both headed her way. Suddenly all the wild tales Veronica liked to tell swirled in her mind. Would they arrest her for trying to speak with the chief of police?

The second man approached. He was tall, distinguished-looking, and perhaps in his forties. His hair was russet with a mingling of gray. "Mrs. . .Montano?" He looked suddenly amused. "I understand you want a word with me."

"Are you Mr. Stephenson?"

"I am."

She glanced at the officer, situated behind his desk once more. "Could we speak privately?"

"Would you mind telling me what this is all about first?"

"It concerns my, um. . .husband."

"I see." A light of understanding flickered in his green eyes. "Follow me."

They walked through the corridor and Stephenson showed her into his office. Two black leather armchairs and a large desk piled with papers comprised most of the small room.

Stephenson closed the door.

"First, why don't you tell me who you really are. And I don't believe the Mrs. Montano bit. . .unless Paden got married in the last week."

"My name is Angelique Huntington. Veronica Huntington and I operate an elite dress shop on the edge of the financial district."

"Ah, I think I know the one. And how is it that you are acquainted with my friend, Paden?"

"Well," Angie began, taking a seat in the chair Stephenson offered, "Paden is Captain Garrett Witherspoon's cousin, and the captain and I were. . .courting."

Nodding, the police chief sat down behind his desk.

"Paden came to me for help last night. He was wounded, you see. . . ." The entire story spilled from Angie's mouth. Several minutes later, she finished and glanced down at her gloved hands, praying she hadn't said too much. When she looked across the wide desk at Stephenson, he seemed deep in thought.

Finally he returned her gaze and sat forward. "I don't see how Paden is at fault if what you just told me is true. He obviously acted in self-defense. And I can vouch for him; he's not a cold-blooded killer. However, there are reasons that this situation must be handled with care and with the utmost discretion." Pursing his lips, he thought a moment longer. "Tell Paden that I'll wire Pinkerton and then, once we find out if Mr. Rosewahl is going to recover, I'll contact him."

"Until then?" Angie asked.

"Until then, he's to stay put."

"But he's in my attic, Sir."

"He'll have to stay there. I'll get his things out of the hotel and have them delivered to your dress shop under the guise of supplies or some such thing."

"I suppose that will be all right." Angie swallowed hard. She'd have to tell Veronica. And Garrett.

As if divining her thoughts, Stephenson added, "And no one else must know about his whereabouts. Is that clear?"

"But what about Paden's cousin? He'll wonder where he is. And what of Veronica, my relative and business partner?"

"You're a sharp lady," Stephenson said, rising to his feet. "Paden wouldn't trust you otherwise. You'll think of something." He chuckled. "*Mrs. Montano.*"

twelve

Angie wasn't pleased with the situation. Not pleased at all. During her entire journey back to the dress shop, she wondered how she would keep Paden hidden from Veronica and Garrett. Then, once she arrived, Veronica informed her that "the good captain" was coming to dinner again tonight.

"You don't mind, do you, Darling?"

"No, no. . .of course not," Angie said reluctantly.

"He's quite amusing."

"Yes, I suppose he is."

"Do you think you'll change your mind about marrying him?"

Angie glanced across the shop at her stepsister. She was studying a swatch of lace at the front counter and appeared disinterested in her question's reply. However, Angie thought there had been a note of. . .something in her tone. Something that countered her impartial demeanor.

"No, I'll not change my mind, *Cinderella*. Prince Charming is all yours."

Veronica's honey-brown head snapped up. "Why, Angelique, you say the most outlandish things!"

She grinned. "You must be rubbing off on me, sister dear."

"I guess I must. But just remember, I'm a widow and widows get away with intrepid behavior."

"So do spinsters," Angie replied, lifting her chin.

Veronica looked aghast. "Spinster?"

"That's what I am, and that's what I'll always be."

"Hmph!" came Veronica's satisfied reply. "You're better

off that way. You'll see."

Angie merely shrugged in silent disagreement before taking up the task of hemming Mrs. Garth's winter wrapper. It was a part of the woman's new wardrobe, purchased for her upcoming journey to London, England, with her husband.

Hours later, Angie and Veronica locked up the dress shop and ambled home, side by side. Upon their arrival, Tu Hing was given immediate orders for tonight's menu, and then Veronica dashed up the stairs to her room, insisting she must dress for dinner. Deciding to seize the opportunity, Angie followed the hired Chinese man into the kitchen.

"Mr. Hing, I'm famished. Could you prepare a plate of food for me?"

He bowed in acquiescence.

"But I'll eat tonight with Veronica and our guest as well."

He gave her a curious glance, but asked no questions. Within minutes, Angie was carrying a plate upstairs to the attic. "Paden," she whispered, announcing her presence, "it's me."

Entering her sewing room, Angie found him sleeping comfortably on the fainting couch. He'd managed to put on his shirt, though he'd torn away the right sleeve. She set down the plate and eyed the wound on his arm, realizing the makeshift bandage was bloodied. Kneeling beside the beige-upholstered lounge, she began carefully unwinding the material.

That's when Paden awoke and considered her through sleepy eyes.

"*Mi angel. . . .*"

Angie frowned at the reference, then touched her fingertips to his forehead. "Oh, no. I think you have a fever."

"I think it is just hot up here," he said with a sleepy grin. "And I am especially warm because I was exercising my arm."

"Yes, I can see that," she murmured, none too pleased,

while inspecting his wound. To her relief, the stitches were still intact. "Paden, you've just got to take it easy."

"*Sí,* I found that out." A shadow of worry darkened his features. "My grip is very weak. I cannot even hold my gun for any length of time. I only pray the strength in this hand will return once my arm heals."

"You might help the Lord out and rest," Angie retorted.

Paden lifted a sardonic brow. "You are as cantankerous as any nurse I have ever known. Perhaps God is calling you to the medical profession."

"Not a chance. I'm happy in the dressmaking business." She stood and searched about for another piece of material to bind Paden's injured arm. When she found a long, cranberry-colored scrap, she knelt back down beside him. "I'm sorry to be so peevish."

"Apology accepted." He paused and Angie could feel the weight of his stare. "You look tired."

"I am, and Veronica invited Garrett to dinner again, so I won't be retiring for the evening any time soon."

"Let me get this straight. The reason for your discontent is because you're being forced to stay up late tonight. . .or is it that my cousin is coming for dinner?"

"Both."

"I see. Well, I'm glad to hear it. For a moment I thought, perhaps, you were angry with me."

Angie shook her head. "Not angry, but I've got bad news from your friend, Chief Stephenson. He says you've got to stay here indefinitely until Mr. Rosewahl's condition is known. Apparently, he is alive, but unconscious." She knotted off the material and sat back on her heels. "Mr. Stephenson said he'll gather your belongings at the hotel and have them sent to our shop. He knows where you are and promised he'd be in touch. Until then, no one else can know you're here."

Paden was momentarily silent as he considered the news. "I hadn't planned on staying here long. I never meant to be such a burden, Angie."

His rueful, dark eyes met hers, melting her heart. "You're not a burden," she said softly. "You're my friend." She smiled. "My *amigo*."

He stroked her cheek with the backs of his fingers. "What if I want to be more than just your friend?"

Angie's eyes widened. "But I thought you had a love interest here in San Francisco."

"I do, and I'm looking at her."

"Me?!" Angie cried, before quickly clapping her hand over her mouth, hoping Veronica hadn't heard the exclamation. After a moment's hesitation, she said, "Paden, you can't be serious."

"I am serious. But you look troubled."

Angie fretted her lower lip as she tried to select the right words. Finally, she decided to be brutally honest. "You're a gunfighter, Paden. I refuse to spend my life with a gunfighter."

"I am not a gunfighter—no more than any other man. I draw on no one, but I must defend myself."

"But your occupation—"

"It is temporary. I want to leave it behind and buy a ranch someplace where there is lush, green grass, cool streams, and tall evergreens. I am so tired of the brown desert."

As Angie listened, she thought it did sound rather inviting. San Francisco had scarcely any trees. Between the building going on within the city and the fire that ravished the land some twenty years ago, there was nary a tree to be found.

"You are thinking about it, *mi amada*."

"No, I'm not," she shot back. "And stop calling me that. . . *mi amada*. . .whatever it means." Angie didn't want to tell him it made her insides all quivery whenever those two words tumbled so eloquently from his lips.

"It is merely an expression of tenderness. Much like if your sister called you 'my dear.' "

"You're not my sister, Paden."

The corners of his mouth lifted, making him look amused. "*Sí,* that's true."

Angie rose from her place on the floor. "I need to dress for dinner," she said, changing the subject. "Garrett will be here soon."

"You are certain that you are not in love with him?"

"I'm certain. And I'm not in love with you, either." She hadn't meant to hurt him, but it was the truth and he needed to hear it.

To her surprise, Paden laughed.

"Shh, Veronica will hear."

"My apologies." He struggled to a sitting position, swung his legs off the fainting couch, and stood. Then he walked slowly toward her. "I know you are not in love with me. . .yet."

"Yet?" She arched her brows in question.

"*Sí,* I mean to charm you, Angie Brown, like you have never been charmed before."

She tried in vain to suppress a little smile. However, she soon realized this wasn't funny. "Paden, don't trifle with me."

"I am not trifling."

She tapered her gaze, gauging his expression. He seemed earnest enough. "Have you prayed about this?" she couldn't help asking.

"I have, and I will continue to pray."

Angie felt somewhat comforted by his reply. "And you really want to start a new life on a ranch?"

Paden nodded. "It is my dream."

She had to admit to being somewhat fascinated. "Will you tell me about it, about this dream of yours?"

"Of course."

"Angelique?" Veronica's voice wafted up the attic stairs. "Are you up there, Dear? It's after six and the captain will be here shortly."

"All right. I'll be down in a moment." She looked back at Paden. "I must go."

"I understand. We will talk later." Taking her hand, he brought her fingers to his lips. "*Hasta la vista*."

Angie felt her knees begin to weaken. "I think you'll make quick work of this charm business," she said, withdrawing her hand.

"*Sí*, I hope so."

Shaking her head at her own gullibility, she strode to the stairwell as Paden's soft chuckle followed in her wake.

❧

Mr. Hing couldn't have prepared a more delectable meal. He had filleted and fried fresh fish and served it with a mound of rice mixed with onions, green peppers, and tomatoes. Garrett was a delightful guest, as usual, but Angie decided his charm couldn't hold a candle to his cousin's. While she ate, she couldn't help daydreaming, wondering what it would be like to marry Paden, leave the confines of the city behind, and live on a ranch. Have children. But could she fall in love with him?

Time would tell.

"Angelique, Dear?"

She snapped from her musings and looked at Veronica.

"The captain asked you a question."

Angie felt her face warm to a blush. "Forgive me. I guess my mind wandered."

"Quite all right." He smiled patiently. "I merely suggested a stroll after dinner."

"The three of us?"

"Ah. . .well. . ." Garrett shifted uncomfortably in his chair.

"You're very kind to offer," Angie went on, "but I'm not up to it. You two go ahead without me."

Two pairs of wide eyes stared at Angie. She blinked back, unsure of what she'd done. Then it struck her; Garrett wanted her company to himself. Angie dabbed at the corners of her mouth with her starched linen napkin and recalled Paden's statement about Garrett being determined to win her hand in marriage. Surreptitiously, she wondered if Garrett knew about his cousin's equivalent goal.

"It is a bit chilly tonight, Captain, don't you think?" Veronica stated politely. "Perhaps we could adjourn to the parlor and play checkers."

Angie had to smile at Garrett's obvious lack of enthusiasm. "Veronica is a marvelous musician," she said. "Maybe we can convince her to play the piano for us."

"I'd like that," he said, glancing Veronica's way.

The woman blushed to her honey-brown hairline. "Angelique, Darling, I don't play that well."

"Of course you do."

Veronica sent her a hooded glance.

Angie returned an innocent smile.

With the meal finished, the three ambled into the parlor, and Veronica grudgingly took her place at the spinet in the far corner. After a few minutes of practice, she began to play a sweet melody that plucked at Angie's heartstrings. "What's the name of this piece?"

The question had been intended for Veronica, but Garrett replied. "It's called 'Lorena,' if I'm not mistaken. It was a song with a powerful punch to Rebel soldiers back in the war. Some became so lonesome when they heard it, they deserted their army."

"You're correct, Captain," Veronica stated with a quick

glance over her shoulder. "It's one of my favorites."

"I've never heard you play it before," Angie remarked curiously.

"That's because it makes me sad. But tonight, for some reason, I felt like playing it." Then Veronica began to sing.

The years creep slowly by, Lorena,
The snow is on the grass again;
The sun's low down the sky, Lorena,
The frost gleans where the flow'rs have been.
But the heart throbs on as warmly now,
As when the summer days were nigh;
Oh! the sun can never dip so low,
A-down affection's cloudless sky.

"That is sad. I think I'm going to cry!" Angie declared, blinking back tears.

Garrett grinned sheepishly before he leaned back, crossed his booted foot to the opposite knee, and stretched his arm across the top of the settee. He appeared, in a word, comfortable. "How is it that a Rebel's song is your favorite, Mrs. Huntington?"

She stopped playing. "Angelique and I hail from Virginia, Captain."

Angie's melancholy vanished, and she laughed softly after glimpsing Garrett's surprised expression.

"Do you mean to tell me that I'm keeping company with Rebel women?" he teased. "I was a Union officer, you know."

"Take heart, Captain," Veronica crooned, "the piece was written by a Northerner and published first in the city of Chicago. Ironic that 'Lorena' was a favorite Confederate love song, don't you think?"

Garrett chuckled heartily. "Ironic, indeed." He glanced at Angie, who was seated across the room. "I'm glad the war is over and I hope never to see another one."

"Amen!" she exclaimed.

Veronica turned back to the piano and played the woeful love song once again, sending a wave of nostalgia crashing over Angie.

Her memories of the war included a sick mother and a ne'er-do-well stepfather. Just before the Civil War began, he got gold fever and moved his entire family to a boomtown in California. Veronica and her husband traveled across the country along with them, and both father and son-in-law panned for gold upon their arrival. Neither ever struck it rich as they'd planned, and both took up diabolical practices, such as drinking and gambling, as they traipsed from one mining town to the next, leaving their families to fend for themselves. Then, after Angie's mother died, her stepfather did the most despicable thing a man can possibly do: He violated his sixteen-year-old stepdaughter. Grievously ashamed and believing that everything wrong in her step-father's life was her fault, Angie never told anyone about the abuse, and she continued to follow him from town to town, saloon to saloon. She was afraid to do otherwise. Finally, he ended up at Chicago Joe's and, in payment for a night of boozing and card playing, he virtually sold Angie into a life of prostitution.

"Veronica, stop playing that song, and don't play it ever again!"

Obviously startled, she paused in midchord, her fingers hovering above the ivory keys, and glanced over at Angie. "Whatever is the matter, Darling?"

"That song evokes horrible memories. Please, stop playing it this instant."

A light of comprehension entered her gaze. "Of course.

Your request is my command. From this moment on, you'll never hear 'Lorena' in this house. How about a game of checkers?" She swivelled around on the piano stool. "Captain, you and I can begin, and the winner will play Angelique."

"All right."

Agreeable as he was, he looked a bit confused by Angie's outburst. She could hardly explain about her jaded past and how it still haunted her at the most inconvenient times. He'd never understand, and in that moment, Angie could only think of one man who would: Paden Montano.

thirteen

"It's been an enjoyable evening, as usual," Garrett said as Veronica handed him his overcoat. "Thank you for inviting me."

"Our pleasure, Captain."

Angie hid a little smile, thinking her stepsister seemed on the verge of falling head over heels in love with the man. She'd caught Veronica gazing at Garrett tonight on several occasions, and there had been no mistaking the stars in her eyes.

"You'll have to come back and visit us soon," Veronica said invitingly.

"Yes, I'd like that." He turned and looked at Angie. "Good night, Angelique."

She effected a tight smile. "There is a matter I wish to discuss with you, Captain. It won't take long. Do you mind?"

"Not at all." In fact, he seemed rather encouraged, much to Angie's dismay.

She grabbed her shawl. "I won't stay out in the night air long," she said to Veronica, whose face fell with disappointment. "I won't be but a moment," she whispered in promise.

Her stepsister merely nodded.

Outside on the porch, Garrett smiled broadly as if he relished this moment alone with her. "What's on your mind? I hope it's the same thing that is on mine."

"I doubt it," Angie replied. She wetted her lips before continuing. "Garrett, why did you lie to me the other day, saying Paden wasn't in his hotel room when he was?"

Garrett looked taken aback by the question. "I. . .well, I. . ." He frowned. "How do you know I lied?"

"Paden told me."

"Perhaps he's the one who's lying."

"Is he?"

Garrett stared at her for several weighted moments, then shook his head. "All right, I'll confess it, for the sin has been pricking my conscience ever since. Yes, I lied. I couldn't seem to help it. The thought of you having anything to do with my cousin causes me to feel insanely jealous."

Angie nibbled her lower lip in consternation. "You need to ask God for strength to get over your jealousy. That's a sin unto itself."

"I know. I know." He glanced off in the distance, then swung his gaze back to her. "My cousin has designs on you, Angelique, in case you haven't noticed."

"Yes, I know," she answered candidly.

"You do?"

She nodded. "He told me."

"He did?" Once the reply registered, Garrett shook his head in irritation. "The knave. Well, I hope you won't be fooled by his philandering ways. He'll leave you brokenhearted, my dear. In fact, I suspect Paden has left town already. I stopped by the hotel late this afternoon and was told at the front desk that he had checked out."

"He'll be back," she stated simply, knowing she couldn't actually dispute the news without giving away important secrets.

"So, you've fallen for him already, eh?" Angie saw an angry muscle work in his jaw. Seconds later, his features relaxed and he stepped closer to her. "You're so young, Angelique," he said softly. "You're young and naive, and of course you'd succumb to Paden's practiced charm."

"You don't know me at all. I'm not as naive as you think. I haven't been a Christian for long and before my conversion I did some things. . .bad things."

"I could give a whit what's in your past. The Bible says

old things pass away, behold all things become new after we accept Christ. I've done some things in my life that I'm not proud of. I'm sure everyone has."

"No, you don't understand. I mean. . .what if you found out I did something horrible. Terrible."

A wry grin curved one side of his mouth. "Like what?"

Angie tried to conjure up something equally as appalling as her former lifestyle. "Well, what would you say if I told you I was once a female outlaw and ran with a murdering gang?"

Garrett dropped his head back and howled with amusement. "I'd say you and Veronica need to stop reading those silly novels." He chuckled again and sat down on the top stair.

Angie lowered herself down beside him, wondering what she could say, other than the truth, to dissuade him. "All right, I wasn't an outlaw," she said, her voice but a whisper, "but I'm not the woman you think I am. I have a. . .a past that I'm ashamed of."

"I told you, the past is the past," he replied in a steady tone, "and I could care less what's in yours. The woman you are today is the one I love."

Angie gulped. She couldn't believe what she was hearing. His words were like a sweet song to her ears. Still, she wasn't beyond the notion that if he really knew what she'd been, he wouldn't be saying he didn't care.

"Does Paden know about your past?"

"Yes. . . ."

Garrett turned to face her. "You told him the details?"

Angie shook her head. "I didn't have to. He knew me back then."

"Excuse me?" His eyes were wide with incredulity.

"I guess it's my turn to confess to some deceit. You see, my mother died, leaving me with a horrid stepfather who abandoned me in Silverstone. Paden was employed by the army and served as the town's sheriff at that time. He was the one who helped me leave and come here to San Francisco. . .and to Veronica." It wasn't the whole truth, but Angie congratulated herself on spilling that much to Garrett.

"Hm," he said, nodding, "this is beginning to make more sense. I had wondered how my cousin could know so much about you in a matter of days."

"I begged him not to tell you anything. When I left Silverstone, I left nothing but wretchedness, and I've worked hard for six years to develop my relationship with the Lord and put my past behind me."

"From what I've heard of Silverstone, I can well imagine your desire to escape it. I'd rather battle the raging sea any day than be stranded in the sun-blanched, untamed territories." Garrett swivelled and took her hand in both of his. "Look, I don't care, Angelique. So you're not from high society. So you were forced to take up residence in a miserable place. All that doesn't matter now. You're born again."

"It shouldn't matter, you're right," Angie countered. "Unfortunately, my past will have lasting effects on me, I'm sure."

"You must put it all behind you, my dear."

Angie knew his suggestion was much easier said than done. "And what would your family say? Would they ever approve of someone like me—a woman with a tarnished history?"

"Is that what you're worried about?" Garrett chuckled. "Well, allow me to put your mind at ease. My family doesn't have to know all the whys and what-fors about your life. It'll stay between the two of us."

"And what if your mother investigates me to be sure I'm a suitable match for her son?"

Garrett shrugged. "We'll get married before we set sail to Maine."

With a long sigh, Angie realized Paden was right: Garrett

wasn't about to take no for an answer. Even a partial truth hadn't deterred him.

"Promise me you'll reconsider, Angelique."

She pulled her hand from his grasp and an image of Veronica flashed across her mind. "I. . .I'm not the woman for you, Garrett."

"Yes, you are. You simply haven't realized it yet."

Angie stood. "All right. I'll reconsider," she said to forestall further debate. "But I can't guarantee I'll change my mind."

"It's enough for me to know you're at least rethinking my offer."

Angie nodded in agreement. "But you have to promise me something in return."

"Anything." His earnestness was endearing if nothing else.

She smiled. "Promise me you'll pray about this matter. . . with an open mind, asking the Lord to specifically show you if we're to marry."

"I promise to do exactly that."

Reaching for her hand, he brought it to his lips, placing a quick kiss on her fingers. Angie became immediately aware that the ardent gesture didn't hold the same effect as Paden's.

"Good night, Angelique."

"Good night," she replied, watching as he descended the rest of the stairs to the street. Turning on her heel, she reentered the house.

❧

Sitting in front of the open attic window, Paden listened to the touching scene taking place two stories below. He knew he shouldn't eavesdrop, but he'd happened upon Angie and Garrett's conversation quite innocently, and now he couldn't seem to tear himself away.

Paden listened as she tried in vain to discourage his cousin, thinking that any man in his right mind would accept the rejection and let it go at that; but Garrett seemed dogged in his quest to win her hand in marriage, while Angie remained ever the diplomat. Another, weaker-willed woman, Paden decided, would most likely succumb to Garrett's impassioned pursuit. He grinned. But not Angie.

However, he heard her agree to reconsider. Was it a measure to put Garrett off, or did she mean it?

A cool ocean breeze sailed in through the window and Paden suddenly became aware of the throbbing in his arm. It tingled and ached right down to his fingertips, indicating obvious nerve damage. He only prayed it would heal. Lifting his arm by taking hold of his wrist, he tucked his hand through two buttons on his shirt, creating a makeshift sling. The pain eased somewhat. Then his side began to hurt where a bullet had grazed him, and he wondered if he'd cracked a rib in the process. His present discomfort combined with thoughts of Angie pushed him to the decision to call it quits with the Pinkerton Agency. He'd had enough gunfights to last a lifetime. It was time to settle down.

He heard footsteps and glanced toward the stairwell, where Angie soon appeared, balancing a large tray. In the other hand, she carried a lighted lamp. Paden smiled a greeting, then met her halfway, taking the lamp from her so as to ease her load. "What did you bring me?"

"Fish and rice," she replied, walking the rest of the way to the sewing room and setting down the tray. She turned and bestowed on him the loveliest of smiles. "Mr. Hing must think I've begun to eat like a moose since this is the second time this evening that I've asked him for a special meal, but I want you to regain your strength."

Paden grinned and placed the lamp on the table near Angie's sewing machine. "I appreciate your efforts."

Angie shrugged, looking a tad embarrassed, and it occurred to Paden that her cheeks suddenly matched the pink flounces and ribbons adorning her white dress. With her blond hair plaited and pinned on top of her head, she reminded Paden of a beautiful princess who'd just stepped from the illustrated pages of a fairy tale. Little wonder his cousin was so besotted with her.

"How's your arm?" she asked with a quizzical frown, seeing his hand inside his shirt.

"It hurts."

"Yes, I imagine. Would a sling help? I could make you one in a matter of minutes."

"*Sí,* Angie, that would help tremendously."

She gave him an accusatory glance. "You haven't been exercising again, have you?"

"No," he said with a grin. Then he raised his right hand. "On my honor I swear that I have been resting just as you instructed."

"Well, good."

Paden had to chuckle. "Does Garry know how bossy you are?"

Angie expelled an indignant huff, causing Paden to laugh all the more. "Shh, Veronica will hear."

"*Lo siento,*" he whispered. "I will try to be more quiet."

Sitting on the fainting couch, he watched as Angie unwound a yardage of material from a bolt, cut it, then began folding it. Next, she walked over to him and draped the fabric around his neck. After a few quick measurements, she took the cloth back to her sewing table and picked up a needle and thread.

"Paden, may I ask you a personal question?"

He debated the reply while watching her expertly weaving the needle in and out of what would soon be his new sling. "You may ask, but I may not be in a position to answer it."

She stopped her sewing and glanced across the room at him. "It's about love."

"What about it?"

"Well. . .how do you know if you're in love or not? I mean, you said you knew I wasn't in love with you. . .yet." She kind of smirked before taking up her needle again. "Are you in love with me, Paden? And if you are, how do you know you are?"

He grinned. "Nothing like a forthright woman to keep a man on his toes," he quipped. He rose and ambled to the window, staring out over the rooftops of San Francisco, trying to select the right words. "Let me see, how can I answer your question? Love, hm?" Turning, he faced her again. "I think love is a many-faceted emotion. Physical attraction, compatibility, and practicality are three of those facets. When I look at you, Angie, I like what I see. I would not mind waking up to find you lying beside me every morning."

"Paden!" She sounded properly chagrined.

"Well, you asked."

"Yes, I did, didn't I?" she muttered.

He chuckled softly, knowing that if she lifted her head from her sewing, he would see that her cheeks were as red as chili peppers. "Now, for compatibility," he continued, "you and I are very compatible. We seem to understand each other in a way that transcends mere interactions. For instance, in a glance I can tell what you feel in your heart. . .and, if I'm not mistaken, you can do the same with me."

She glanced at him, obviously calculating his words.

"As for practicality, you want to have a family, Angie, and I am more than ready to settle down. I am a man who adheres to his commitments and I am a Christian, so when I promise to be faithful, you can be assured I mean it. I'm also a capable man, and I'll earn a good living. I was reared on a ranch, so I know about horses, cattle, the annual drives, and the hard work." He paused before adding, "And if you don't know how to cook yet, you're smart enough to learn. I am not worried that I'll starve to death."

"Very funny," she shot at him. "For your information, I cook very well."

"See? There you have it. A future together is meant to be."

Angie tied off the thread, then lifted her scissors and cut it from the material. Rising from the wooden chair, she crossed the room and fitted him with his new sling. With his injured arm tightly secured now, he felt the pain slowly subside.

"Paden," Angie began, "your definition of love sounds too impersonal to me. You can't select a wife like you'd select a prized calf. There's got to be some feeling behind it—and more than mere physical attraction."

"True love takes time to cultivate, to grow and blossom."

She stared up at him, her blue eyes searching his face, searching for answers he didn't possess.

"Follow your heart, *querida*," he said, fingering several silky, gold strands near her temple which had come loose from their pinning. Then suddenly, he longed to kiss her, except he vividly recalled her adverse reaction to his cousin taking such liberties, and quickly squelched the desire. He was not, by nature, a patient man; however, he would bide his time for Angie's sake, so as not to scare her off.

"Have you ever been in love?" she asked, still gazing up at him sweetly.

He grinned. "I don't believe so. . .unless, of course, you want to count the time when I was seven and terribly infatuated with my schoolteacher, Margarita Benicia Carrillo. Alas, she broke my heart and ran off with one of the ranch hands."

Angie's eyes sparkled with amusement and when she smiled, it was as if the room filled with sunshine. Paden wondered if it would be so easy to bide his time after all.

As if divining his thoughts, she took a step backward. "I should go and leave you to eat your meal in peace."

Paden replied with a single nod.

"But, do you want to know a secret, first?"

"What's that?" he said, thoroughly enchanted by the young woman standing before him.

"I think Veronica has developed feelings for Garrett."

Paden raised curious brows. "Is that right?"

"Yes. I'd ask her about love, except I don't think she's inclined to discuss the subject. Not yet. But if I could get Garrett to—"

"Ah-ah-ah," he cut in on a warning note. "Do not play the matchmaker, or you will be sorry."

"I don't intend to play matchmaker," she replied indignantly. "I just want to help things along a bit."

"Stay out of the way, Angie. You will only hurt the ones you love by interfering. If God wants Garry and your stepsister together, He will work out the details. In fact, He has already."

She weighed his words, then nodded. "You're right. I guess I'm a romantic at heart."

Paden couldn't help teasing her. "Well, I am not a man opposed to romance. Save your antics for me."

She gave him a quelling look, and he laughed.

"Shh!"

"My apologies," he whispered.

"Angelique?"

Her eyes widened, and beneath the glow of lamplight, she resembled a little girl caught in the act of snitching a second cookie. "Coming, sister dear," she finally replied.

"I heard a man's voice up there."

Angie grimaced. "Um. . .it must have come from outside. Perhaps you heard Mr. Hing. In any case, I'll be right down." Whispering, she told Paden, "I'll have to take my lamp. It'll look suspicious if I show up without it."

"Do not worry. I have the one you brought up last night if I feel like reading. Otherwise, the moonlight coming through the window is bright enough by which to eat."

"All right, then." She gave him a parting smile. "Good night."

"Good night, Angie. Sleep well."

As he watched her departure, he felt oddly remorseful. He would miss her challenging inquisitions and delightful company. Her smile. Her twinkling, blue eyes. He hoped she would not stay away too long.

He moved toward the tray she'd left and had to grin at the sudden irony. He might have set out to charm Angie Brown, but it was she who had somehow taken hold of his heart.

And then he wondered if this is what it felt like to fall in love.

fourteen

Veronica could not be placated; she insisted she had heard a man's voice in the attic. "It's him, Angelique. It's Billy!"

"No, it's not. I was just up there, and I promise I didn't see or hear that horrid man." Angie sighed. "He's dead, Veronica. He can't come back and haunt you. It's impossible."

"Then I'm going mad."

"No, no, there's a reasonable explanation for what you heard."

"What is it?"

Angie fretted over her lower lip, hovering between honesty and loyalty. "I can't tell you right now," she replied at last. "Please, don't ask me why. I promised I wouldn't say."

Veronica's features relaxed, and she suddenly appeared almost excited. "Is it a. . .a surprise?"

"Well, yes."

"Oh, I just love surprises! What are you up to, Angelique?"

"I told you, I can't say."

"Who are you hiding up in the attic? A carpenter? Is he restoring that old desk of my mother's—the one I'm so fond of? It's a sight for sore eyes, isn't it? It fell off the wagon twice on the journey across the country. Billy swore if it fell off a third time, he'd chop it to pieces and use it for kindling."

Angie inadvertently glanced at the ceiling, wondering if Paden could make himself useful and refinish wood, even though he could use only one arm.

"All right, Angelique. I'll let you have your fun. I won't snoop or question you further, but it is quite late for a man to be working in our house. I hope he doesn't plan to stay much longer."

She chuckled. "Oh, I can't fathom how you snuck a man in here, right under my nose. Mr. Hing must be in on your little secret." She laughed once more. "You're such a dear thing."

Angie produced a tiny smile and watched her stepsister retire to her room. She felt clammy from the stress of Veronica's interrogation. Short of lying, Angie didn't know how much longer she could hide Paden.

Entering her own room, she folded down the bedcovers, then began her nightly routine. Perhaps tomorrow, she thought, unpinning her hair, she would hear from Mr. Stephenson, and he'd tell her that Paden could safely be freed. As she picked up her silver-handled brush, she wondered why she felt a twinge of disappointment.

❧

"Look what I brought for you ladies!" Garrett boomed as he entered the dress shop the next morning. "You're always feeding me, so I decided to return the favor."

Angie looked up from her hemming. "It smells delicious, whatever it is."

Veronica stood from the table at which she'd been sitting, scouring the latest Butterick pattern book, and met him at the door. "Cinnamon. I smell cinnamon."

"Indeed you do, Mrs. Huntington. And I've been told that these are the best frosted cinnamon rolls in the entire city."

"How thoughtful of you, Captain. Please come in." She turned. "Angelique, please set the tea kettle to boiling."

Angie lay aside the gown on which she'd been sewing and made her way to the back room. Just as she arrived, someone in the alley pounded on the back door. She turned to Mr. Lee, who dutifully answered it.

"I have a delivery for a Mrs. . .um. . ." The kind-faced, hired man, who appeared as though he might be someone's beloved grandfather, opened the order slip in his hand. "Mrs. Paden Montano."

"No one here by that name," the bulky security guard replied, closing the door.

"Wait!" Angie said. She gave Mr. Lee an embarrassed, little smile. "I know who that is. I'll accept the delivery."

He had the good grace not to ask, but assisted the older man with a valise. The contents, Angie suspected, were Paden's belongings from the hotel. Now how in the world was she supposed to get them from here to the house?

"Mr. Lee, would you mind terribly storing this large satchel in the far corner back there? I'll retrieve it later."

He silently nodded his acquiescence.

Angie peered out the curtained threshold to find Veronica and Garrett chatting amicably. She sighed with relief. At least they'd been preoccupied these past minutes, but how was it that Chief Stephenson sent something to *Mrs.* Paden Montano. That creature didn't exist. Although Angie had to admit, the name had a nice ring to it.

The water came to a boil and Angie finished preparing the tea before carrying it out on a large tray. Reaching the table, she set down her burden and placed cups and saucers in front of Veronica first, then Garrett. Next, she began to pour the tea, but when her gaze met the captain's angry stare, she gasped and missed his cup, spilling onto the table. Angie quickly soaked it up with one of the linen napkins on the tray.

"Mrs. Huntington just informed me of your little endeavor to surprise her. Is it true, Angelique, that you're harboring a man in your attic?"

She felt the blood drain from her face.

"He's working on Mother's desk. I'm sure of it," Veronica interjected. "I always guess secrets."

Angie laughed, but it sounded nervous to her own ears. "You shouldn't have told Garrett, you silly thing. Now he won't be surprised, either."

She chanced a look at him and he narrowed his gaze

suspiciously. Suddenly Angie felt like her corset was much too tight.

"I, um, think I forgot something in the back room. Please excuse me."

She turned to go, but Garrett stood and quickly caught her elbow. "I think you need a bit of air, Angelique. You look rather. . .peaked." Before she could reply, he propelled her from the shop.

"Unhand me," she hissed.

He ignored her and led her down the boardwalk, past several curious pairs of eyes.

"You're hurting me, Garrett, and you're making a scene."

They rounded the corner and he stopped, placed his hands on her shoulders, and gave her a mild shake. "Where's Paden?"

"How should I know?"

"What are you up to?"

"Nothing."

"Who's in your attic?"

Angie swallowed the humiliation threatening to well in her eyes. "Veronica thinks the ghost of her late husband is up there. I've tried to tell her otherwise—"

"What do you take me for, a fool?"

At his harsh tone, Angie couldn't contain her tears any longer.

"Angelique, I want the truth."

"I. . .I can't tell you," she sniffled in reply.

Garrett straightened, and Angie realized she'd forgotten what an imposing figure he made. "If you won't tell me, I'll just have to find out for myself."

Pivoting, he took off walking in the direction of her home, and Angie debated whether he'd actually barge into their private residence and search the attic. But then, knowing his jealous temperament, she decided he would, and she made the choice to go after him.

"Garrett, wait. Please." He kept up his pace, and Angie had to trot to catch up. "I can explain everything."

Garrett refused to reply, although she saw an angry muscle work in his jaw. They neared her street, rounding another corner, and within minutes, Garrett was marching up to the front door with Angie, feeling winded, coming up behind him. He held out his hand. "I want your key."

"I don't have it," she replied honestly, breathlessly. "It's at the shop."

Garrett knocked loudly on the wooden door, while Angie prayed Mr. Hing was away at the market. Unfortunately, he answered, fulfilling his role as an occasional butler. To Angie's horror, Garrett pushed his way past the Chinese man, who began muttering in annoyance.

"It's all right, Mr. Hing," she tried to assure him, except she wasn't certain anything was "all right" at the present moment.

In reply, the dedicated employee shuffled angrily into the kitchen. Angie strode into the parlor and collapsed into an armchair. Moments later, she heard Garrett's thundering voice; he'd obviously found Paden. Then all was eerily quiet, and Angie hoped the two men hadn't killed each other.

Her temples began to throb. Leaning back in the chair, she rubbed them in a circular motion with her fingertips. Unfortunately, the throbbing soon became a pounding, and her laudanum was in the attic with Paden.

"Angelique?" Veronica's voice hailed her from the foyer. "Are you here, Angelique?"

"In the parlor."

Veronica sailed through the doorway. "I'm so glad I found you here. I was so worried, I closed the shop for the morning. Whatever is going on? Why was the captain acting so strangely?"

Angie stood, trying to ignore her brain-twisting headache. "Come along, I'll show you why."

Taking her stepsister's hand, she led her up one flight of stairs, but when they came to the steps to the next floor, Veronica balked.

"I am not going up there, Angelique."

"Yes, you are. There's nothing to be afraid of. I'll be right beside you, and Garrett is up there along with. . .well, you'll soon find out."

"But the ghost—"

"There is no such thing. Now it's time to face your fears, sister dear. Soon you'll see you've been afraid of nothing for years."

Grudgingly, Veronica ascended the steps. "At least I'm facing my fears in broad daylight," she muttered.

They reached the attic, and Angie felt her stepsister's grip tighten around her hand. "Don't be afraid."

Veronica gave her a skeptical glance, but Angie continued onward to the sewing room. They walked in, disturbing a discussion; however, Angie was pleased to see both men acting calm and civil, even though she hadn't forgiven Garrett for his gruff behavior.

Veronica gasped. "Why, Mr. Montano, what are you doing here? And your arm. . .whatever has happened?"

Angie sent Paden an apologetic look. "I couldn't keep your presence a secret any longer. I'm so sorry."

"Do not worry, *mi amada*. It could not be helped."

"What's going on?" Veronica asked once more.

"I'll let Paden explain," Angie said, spying the brown bottle of laudanum on the sewing table, adjacent to the fainting couch. She crossed the room and picked up her medicine. "By the way," she told Paden, "Chief Stephenson dropped your belongings off at the shop. They're in a valise in the back room." She glanced around the tiny group. "Now, if you'll excuse me, I must lie down. I've acquired one of my sick headaches."

"Of course, Darling," Veronica replied.

"Angelique, may I have a word with you before you leave?" Garrett asked.

"No, you may not," she snapped. "And I hope to never speak to you again!" With that, Angie spun on her heel and ran for the sanctuary of her bedroom.

fifteen

Paden relaxed on the settee in the parlor in the company of his cousin and Mrs. Huntington. It was nice to be out of seclusion, although he sorely missed Angie. She had remained in her room, nursing a headache, causing him some concern; but her stepsister insisted Angie's "sick headaches" were a fairly common occurrence and that she usually recovered within twenty-four hours.

"Would you like some coffee, Mr. Montano? Captain?" Paden politely declined, but Garrett accepted a cup. Veronica relayed the order to her Chinese employee.

"The meal was delicious," Garrett remarked.

"Sí, gracias," Paden agreed. "Scrumptious fare, to be sure."

Veronica blushed prettily. "Oh, well, you're both quite welcome. But I enjoyed our dinner conversation the best." She turned to Garrett. "It seems I've developed a fascination for ships. Thank you for answering all my silly questions."

He smiled broadly. "Glad to oblige. Ships and the sea are two of my favorite topics."

Paden tried to conceal his mirth. It seemed Angie was right: Her sister did appear romantically interested in Garry.

He studied the two and thought they made a handsome couple. Both were kindhearted souls, although Veronica was still in need of salvation. Even so, had it not been for her compassion in seeing to it that Paden obtained his valise from the dress shop this afternoon, he would not be clothed in a fresh shirt and trousers tonight. And Garry. . .he had been extremely concerned about Paden's wounds. So concerned, in fact, he forgot how angry he was that Paden had been hiding out in the Huntingtons' attic.

"It's such a shame Angelique didn't feel well enough to join us this evening," Garrett said. Sitting across the room from Paden, he shook his head. "I feel just awful. I acted like a veritable brute this morning."

Paden wasn't about to argue, having heard his cousin's side of the story. Little wonder Angie didn't want to speak to him.

"If she wasn't quite so spirited and independent, I wouldn't get so angry," Garrett mused aloud. "But I know she's young. . . ."

"Garry, your anger is your problem, not Angie's."

Garrett clenched his jaw in reply, although he appeared to be considering the remark.

"On the other hand, the captain is right. Angelique is somewhat vivacious and individualistic, but that's her creative nature," Veronica informed the men. "She has the most unique notions, and she's very talented with a needle and thread. Why, Huntington House Dress Shop was her brilliant idea. There I was, a widow with dwindling funds, unsure of what to do with the rest of my life. Then Angelique showed up at my door in need of a place to stay. . .why, she gave purpose to my life again."

Suddenly, a knock sounded at the front door. A look of surprise flashed across Veronica's face before she excused herself to answer it. When she left the room, Garrett shook his head, his expression one of disappointment. "Angelique needs a man with a firm hand to curb that independence of hers."

Paden chuckled. "I rather like an independent woman."

Garrett snorted. "Have you not read in the Scriptures that a wife is to submit to her husband?"

"Yes, but if I recall the passage correctly, the apostle Paul prefaces his instructions to wives by saying that both spouses must submit themselves to one another in the fear of God."

Paden grinned. "Husbands have their own share of submitting to do—which was quite difficult for me to understand at first. You see, the home in which I grew up was quite patriarchal. My father was the ruler and my mother was to obey his every word. While he loved her deeply—still does—he could be a tyrant. Of course, he has tempered with age. But my mother was a bit like Angie, idealistic and independent, and I remember as a child—" He shook his head. "Ai-yai-yai! The sparks would fly between my parents."

"That's because she didn't submit to her husband."

"Partly true. But my father submitted to no one either. . . not even to the Lord."

Garrett sat back, looking agitated. He folded his muscular arms across his chest. "So what's your point, *Cousin?*"

"My point is that there must be a give and take in marriage. It cannot be so one-sided as one orders, the other obeys."

"Yeah? What makes you such an expert? You know no more about marriage than I do."

"True, but I know women. I lived with my mother and sisters, and I know a man has to approach females in a careful way if he hopes for a good response."

"All right, I agree with that much. But my 'approach,' as you call it, is much different than yours."

"*Sí,* it is—and look how Angie responds. If I may remind you, *Cousin*, she is currently not speaking to you."

Garrett opened his mouth in rebuttal, but Veronica suddenly appeared at the doorway. "Mr. Montano, the chief of police is here to see you." She looked a bit flustered. "He says he'd like to speak with you. . .in private."

Paden rose from his place on the settee. "Thank you, Mrs. Huntington," he said with a slight bow.

"I hope there's no trouble."

He gave her an assuring smile. "Do not fret. Andy Stephenson is a friend of mine."

"A friend?" She looked over her shoulder at her uniform-clad guest before turning back to him. "Oh. Well, then. . ." She smiled, looking both curious and concerned. "I'll leave you two to your conversation."

"Gracias."

Stepping into the front hallway, Paden grinned at the sight of his longtime friend standing by the door.

"*Amigo*," he greeted, "I would shake your hand, but as you can see, my right arm is in a sling and is temporarily out of commission."

Stephenson smirked. "Forget the handshake. I'm just happy to see you're alive."

"*Sí*, me, too."

The two men walked farther into the foyer so they wouldn't be overheard. "Listen, Pal," Andy began seriously, "I won't mince words; you need to get out of town. Fast. Rosewahl died this afternoon, and his son is distraught. He personally told me that he's looking to kill you and kill everything you love—just like you killed his father.

"Now, look, Paden, I've conducted an impromptu investigation, and I've found that Rosewahl and Littleton were involved in a mining speculation scheme. Rosewahl's bank was more or less the cover for the whole operation. Munson got involved when he came to town with his ill-gotten gains. Anyone with no conscience and a lot of money was welcome to join. When I told young Frank Rosewahl about the conspiracy, he refused to believe it and threatened to kill me, too, so I locked him up. But I don't know how long I can keep him behind bars. He's already hollering for his attorney, and our police force has many San Francisco residents suspicious because of lies and rumors that originated from men like Rosewahl and Littleton. They were in the upper echelon of society, well-respected in the business district by day and veritable thieves by night. Therefore, if I keep Frank in jail and his lawyer decides to smear our reputation further, we could end up with riots."

"I understand. Let him go," Paden replied, leaning against the balustrade at the foot of the staircase. "I have faced dangerous men who have wanted to kill me before. I'm not afraid. I will not run like a coward."

"But you can't defend yourself. You're injured."

Paden knew he had a point there.

"Look, my friend, take my advice. Get out of San Francisco, marry that little imp you sent into my station, and settle down somewhere."

"Little imp?" He grinned. "You mean Angie?"

Stephenson chuckled. "I do, indeed. She walked into the station and, in order to get around one of my officers, announced herself as Mrs. Paden Montano. When the news got out, it caused quite a few chuckles among my men who know you."

Paden grinned broadly, feeling oddly encouraged. "*Sí,* I'm sure it did. To tell you the truth, I have already proposed marriage to Angie and she is. . .considering my offer."

"So, you know this woman?"

He nodded.

Stephenson frowned. "How well do you know her?"

Paden lifted a brow. "I beg your pardon?"

"Well," he drawled, leaning against the wall and folding his arms across his chest, "after *Mrs. Montano* left the station, I did a little snooping and discovered she's got a couple of aliases. Her real name is Angela Sarah Brown, also known in San Francisco as Angelique Huntington."

"I know all about Angie's past."

"I figured maybe you did." Stephenson rubbed his jaw contemplatively. "But if you care a whit about this lady, you'll get her out of San Francisco before Frank Rosewahl's attorney digs up the same information and ruins her name and her reputable dressmaking business. The two of you have been linked together. You've been seen around town. Your first mistake was taking her into Tibbles' Café. That's the gossip capital of the Golden Gate. One of the serving girls reported seeing you and Miss Huntington engrossed in an intimate chat."

Paden sighed. He recalled the afternoon clearly. Angie had admitted that she didn't love Garrett, and it was then that Paden had begun to think along the lines of winning her heart for himself.

"What I'm trying to say is, if Rosewahl's attorney doesn't slander the Huntington name, Frank might harm her to get to you."

"Harm Angie?" He narrowed his gaze. "Young Rosewahl would be signing his own death warrant if he so much as touches a single hair on her head."

"You got it bad, don't you?" One corner of Stephenson's mouth went up slightly. "I can hardly believe my ears. I guess you're serious about this woman."

"I am serious. Very serious," Paden said with absolute certainty.

Stephenson leaned forward. "Then get out of town and take her with you."

He sighed. "I can't leave San Francisco. I haven't finished my job. I haven't let Allan Pinkerton down yet, and I don't plan to start now. I must apprehend Harry Munson."

"Munson?" Stephensón shook his head. "That man is probably long gone, and you can't ride off on a manhunt with a lady in tow. It's one or the other."

After inhaling deeply, Paden let out a long, slow breath.

"What's it gonna be?"

"All right, all right. I don't know how, but I promise that by this time tomorrow, Angie and I will have left San Francisco."

❧

"There's got to be another way!"

Paden sighed as he knelt before Angie, taking her hand in his. "Believe me, I thought of everything, including sending you to my family in Mexico. Unfortunately, that idea presents its own share of problems—the foremost being your travel from the coast to the ranch on which my father is foreman. It would not be safe. Finally, I shared the dilemma with Garry, and his suggestion makes the most sense."

"But I don't want to sail to Maine with him. Not only do I not love him, but I've decided that I don't even like him."

Paden smiled warmly, revealing white, even teeth, a contrast to his brown skin and swarthy features. "I am glad to hear that."

"This isn't funny, and it's not a game of win or lose."

He sobered. "You are right." He squeezed her hand gently, his forearm now resting on her knee. "Still, I think it's the only way. You will be safe and your reputation will be spared."

Tears filled Angie's eyes as everything inside her screamed against this plan. "Paden, I get awfully seasick."

"Garry says he knows of medicine you can take. He will purchase it for you at the apothecary before you set sail."

"But I don't want to go."

Paden sighed once more. "I'm afraid you have no choice."

"What about if I leave town by way of the stagecoach?"

"And where will you go?"

Angie's heart sank. She didn't have a reply. Beseeching him with her misty gaze, she said, "Can't I go with you. . .wherever you're going?" His moment's hesitation gave her reason enough to continue. "A ranch sounds very nice. I can cook, and I'm a hard worker. You said, yourself, that it's a practical solution. You want to settle down and I want a family."

"Unfortunately, I have a job to finish before I can make that dream become a reality."

Angie swallowed, feeling wounded by his words. "So what you're saying is, your job is more important to you than I am." She yanked her hand from his and stood, then strode to the parlor windows, her arms crossed in front of her.

"You are not making this easy."

"Easy?" She spun on her heel. "I am in peril because of you. This is your fault, and now, in spite of all your sweet-talk, you're deserting me. On second thought, it's worse than desertion. You're putting me on a horrible ship of all things! But that's just fine," she said, swatting at an errant tear, "because you will never be more than a gunfighter, Paden. You just proved it."

She marched out of the room and ran up the stairs, nearly colliding with Veronica in the hallway. Glimpsing her stepsister's troubled expression, Angie's tears burst forth unchecked. "I'm so sorry," she choked. "I never wanted to ruin the Huntington name."

"Don't be silly," Veronica replied with tears of her own. "You couldn't ruin it any more than my late husband. It's a respectable name because of you. . .us. Our shop."

Angie lowered her gaze, uncertain as to how to reply. On one hand, she appreciated Veronica's compliment, but on the other, she felt ashamed of her past.

"You know," Veronica said, using her lace hanky to dab her eyes, "you and I could set up shop somewhere else. I mean, there are other large cities and some with plenty more females than this one."

Angie blinked, feeling suddenly hopeful.

"And we're East Coast women, Angelique, born in Virginia."

"You want to go back to Virginia?"

Veronica shook her head. "There's nothing for us there anymore, but Maine. . .that is, we wouldn't have to go all the way to Maine, but if the ship is headed that way, perhaps we could get off in New York."

"New York. . ." Angie thought the plan had possibilities. New York was a fashion-conscious city if ever one existed.

"Should I find the captain and ask if he'll book passage for me, too?"

"Yes!" Angie exclaimed, hugging her stepsister around the shoulders. "Oh, but, on second thought. . .could we travel by stagecoach?"

"Darling, I would never survive the trip."

Angie wasn't convinced that she'd outlive the journey by sea; however, unlike Veronica, she had the Lord to rely on for grace and strength. Somehow she would manage.

"I can't believe that you're willing to leave your home for me."

"This place? With its haunted attic?" Veronica sniffed in mock indignation. "I will be glad to get rid of it." She became thoughtful for a moment, then looked as if she were making a mental list. "I'll have to hire an agent to sell the house and liquidate our shop."

"There are trunks upstairs."

"Gracious me! We've got a million things to do before we board this evening."

Angie grinned.

"First, I must find Captain Witherspoon." Veronica headed purposely for the stairwell.

"Tell him that I will not go without you."

She tossed a smile over her shoulder. "I'll be sure to relay the message."

sixteen

Paden found Angie's aloofness quite disturbing, and it didn't help matters that his cousin gloated over the situation's outcome. "She's not talking to you either, Garry," Paden reminded him as they sat alone at the dinner table while the ladies packed their belongings upstairs.

"Ah, yes, but I have approximately two months to remedy that little matter."

His cousin's remark caused Paden to bristle. "Just remember, New York is now the Huntington women's final destination."

Garrett chuckled. "I have two months in which to correct that, too."

But could he? Paden had to wonder. Angie had seemed adamant about her feelings for Garry. Would she change her mind?

Just then something his mother liked to say flashed across his memory. *It's a woman's prerogative to change her mind.* The phrase used to infuriate Paden's father, largely because he knew with that kind of disclaimer, he'd never get the same answer one day to the next, and with five women in the house, that got to be quite disturbing.

Well, Paden wasn't going to take that chance with Angie. He needed some sort of pledge from her or he'd likely be *loco* for the next eight weeks.

"Excuse me," he said, wiping his mouth with his linen napkin before placing it on the table. He slid his chair back and stood. "I have some unfinished business to take care of."

Garrett shrugged. "Of course."

Walking away from the dining room, he thought he might like

to physically wipe the satisfied sneer off his cousin's face. Pausing at the foot of the steps, he listened to the goings-on above him, noting the excitement in Veronica's voice and the dread in Angie's. She hated traveling by ship, but perhaps she'd fare better on this journey than the one she'd taken six years ago. Regardless, he couldn't let Angie board in a matter of hours, believing he cared about his job more than he cared about her. But how could he convince her otherwise? What could he possibly say? What could he give her? What promise could he make? And why did he feel so desperate to do. . .*something?*

Paden knew the answer to the latter; simply, it tore him up inside to imagine Angie married to his cousin or any other man. Taking the stairs two at a time, he reached the top landing and put his forefinger over his lips to silence Mrs. Huntington, who'd gasped in surprise at seeing him. "I need to have a few words with Angie," he whispered.

"Well, to be honest," she whispered back, "I don't know if she'll allow it."

"I have to try."

Hesitantly, Veronica nodded.

Walking the rest of the way to Angie's room, he strode in unannounced and closed the door behind him. He took in the sight of Angie, dressed in a fawn-colored traveling suit, her blond hair coiled at her nape, and he couldn't recall ever seeing a lovelier woman.

"Veronica, I—" Angie turned around, garments dangling over her arm, and inhaled sharply. "You! What are you doing here? Get out this instant!"

"I will leave as soon as I have my say."

After an indignant little huff, she gave him a look of acquiescence. "Very well, what is it?"

Paden stepped forward, feeling less surefooted than he had a moment ago. "Now that I have your attention, I am not sure how to begin."

She gave him a perturbed little frown.

"I don't think there were ever words created to express how I feel, what I must tell you."

Her expression turned from aggravated to curious.

"I loathe the idea of you sailing out of San Francisco because I know it will be months before I see you again. Yet, I cannot think of a better escape for you. I am comforted somewhat to know your stepsister will now join you, and my cousin will be a capable escort. But I will. . .miss you, Angie."

"You will?" she asked skeptically.

"*Sí,* I will. I only hope and pray that you will miss me half as much."

In reply, she glanced at the gowns draped over her forearm.

"And you are wrong about my job. It is not more important than you," Paden said, hoping to put all her doubts to rest. "But I have an obligation, and completing this assignment fulfills my obligation to Allan Pinkerton. Only then will I be free to begin a new life, a new career. Can you even try to understand why I cannot walk away, or in this case, sail away from my work? I must finish what I have begun."

She met his gaze, and Paden's insides twisted at the sight of the anguish in her blue eyes.

"Finishing this job means another gunfight," she said, "and next time you might not emerge the victor. Next time, you might be killed."

"It's always a possibility," Paden admitted. "But will you pray for me—pray for my protection?"

She weighed her reply. "Yes, I'll pray."

Encouraged, Paden took another step closer to her. "Will you wait for me, Angie? Will you promise not to marry someone else during the interim? As soon as I apprehend Munson and surrender him to the proper authorities, I will come to New York and find you. We will then resume our. . .um. . . courtship."

"Some courtship," she muttered.

"I will make it up to you."

She searched his face, gauging his words. "I have never known you to lie."

"I am not a liar, Angie. Besides, if I didn't love you, I would not feel so troubled about your departure, yet I know there is no other recourse."

She appeared momentarily stunned. "What did you say?"

"I said, I am not lying. . . ."

"No, no, after that. You said—" She blinked. "Did you say you loved me?"

Paden paused, realizing that's exactly what he'd said. Where had those words come from, except from his heart? "*Sí*, Angie, I love you," he said, knowing now he meant every word of it.

She tossed the dresses onto a nearby chair. "When? When did you know you loved me? How?"

Paden had to chuckle at her bewildered expression. "I don't know when or how, I just know that's the way I feel. And you? How do you feel about me?"

She thought a moment before narrowing her gaze. "I feel like I could shoot you myself for all the upheaval you've caused me."

With his right arm still in a sling, he managed to lift his hand to his heart. "Such words of ardor," he quipped.

She had the good grace to look chagrined. Then, on a more serious note, she said, "I honestly don't know how I feel. You will always be special to me because you helped me escape Silverstone, but I'm unsure if that constitutes love."

He nodded, disappointment swelling in his chest. But what had he expected? Closing the distance between them, he slipped his uninjured arm around her waist and pulled her close to him. To his relief, she didn't recoil. "How many men have told you they loved you, Angie, hm?" he fairly whispered against her velvety-soft cheek.

She half laughed, half grunted at the question. "Scores of men, most of them drunkards." The reply had a bitter sound.

Paden drew his head back slightly. "I think if I were in your position, I would not believe another man who touted those three little words, 'I love you.' How empty they must sound."

Tears sprang into her eyes, and Angie tried in vain to blink them away.

"And yet, you long to hear those words—no, you long to *believe* those words, believe the man who is saying them, don't you?"

Angie nodded, her gaze lowered, her fingers fidgeting with the fraying hem of his sling.

"So it is up to me to prove my love to you, and I gladly accept the challenge. All I ask is that you wait for me. Wait for a just a little while. Until Christmas. Can you promise me that?"

Still misty-eyed, she nibbled her lower lip in contemplation while Paden held an anxious breath. At last she nodded out a subtle, but affirmative, reply.

"So you give me your promise that you'll wait?"

"Yes," she said. "I give you my promise."

"And you will board the clipper with no complaints?"

"Yes, yes. . . ."

"Good. And I promise you, Angie, you will not be sorry."

She smiled, albeit weakly, and Paden longed to kiss her tremulous, strawberry pink lips and taste of their sweetness, but instead he stepped backward. Far be it for him to lose Angie's confidence now by succumbing to physical desire. No doubt, she'd been the recipient of such contrived devotion before. Even Garrett had taken something from her that she wasn't yet ready to give.

Backing up to the door, Paden bowed courteously. "We

have an understanding then, *sí*?"

Angie suddenly appeared completely at ease. She smiled, and this time it heightened the hue of her eyes. "*Sí, señor.* We have an understanding."

❧

Angie couldn't believe how lighthearted she felt after Paden left the room. It was as if a huge weight had been lifted from her, setting her spirit free again. Perhaps her anger with Paden, her disappointment in him, had been the albatross around her neck. Regardless, she found herself greatly respecting the man now. He had somehow comprehended the deepest part of her, and metaphorically, he had touched upon a place where no man had ever dared. All that, and Paden hadn't even kissed her—even though she had found herself wanting to be kissed. Quite a surprise, since Angie never imagined herself longing for a man's lips to touch her own.

"Angelique?" Veronica stepped into the room, forcing Angie from her sweet reverie. "Is everything all right?"

"Oh, yes." Oddly, she felt herself begin to blush.

"Mr. Montano didn't upset you further, did he?" Veronica seated herself, smoothing out the skirt of her brown tweed, two-piece traveling dress.

"No." Angie stared at the mirror and hairbrush in her hand before setting them into the trunk. Peeking at her stepsister from beneath lowered lashes, she added, "Paden said he loves me."

Veronica lifted a pert brow. "Is that so? Well, add another man to the list. It gets longer every day."

Angie laughed softly at the retort.

"And if I recall, the captain's name is there among the others."

"Yes, but this is different, sister dear. Paden means it."

"The others don't? Surely Captain Witherspoon is as smitten as they come."

"But don't you see? He, like others, said he loves me solely because he wants to possess me and force me to be someone I'm not, nor ever will be. Paden, on the other hand, knows and accepts me for who I am—like you did when I showed up on your doorstep so many years ago."

"Hm, I've never heard you talk this way before."

"I've never felt this way before."

"This sounds serious and, goodness, I believe I see stars in your eyes!"

Angie laughed heartily at the remark, while Veronica chuckled along with her.

"Ladies?" Garrett's voice reverberated up the staircase. "We need to leave shortly."

All amusement vanished, and the frenzy of gathering belongings and packing trunks resumed.

At last, neither Angie nor Veronica could get another item into the three trunks they had between them. Paden and Garrett made three separate trips upstairs, each man taking an end of a large trunk, then another, and another, carrying them out to the awaiting carriage. In the parlor, Veronica gave Mr. Hing last minute instructions. He could remain on the premises until the agent sold the house, and he was to guard existing assets. Furthermore, Veronica urged him to get a message to Mr. Lee at the shop. The agent would take care of handling the merchandise, but Mr. Lee needed to be informed. With each command, the Chinese man bowed courteously, and Angie felt sad to leave him behind. If she wasn't mistaken, he looked a bit sorrowful, himself.

"Time to go," Garrett announced.

Stepping outside into the evening dusk, Angie glanced around for Paden. He couldn't have left already, not without saying good-bye. Or had they said their good-byes?

Suddenly she spied him on the far side of the carriage, astride his black stallion. He had taken his arm out of the sling and, clad in ebony trousers, vest, overcoat, and wide-brimmed hat, he looked very much like the handsome sheriff who had helped her escape Chicago Joe's house of ill-fame. How ironic that she was running away from her past for a second time. Well, she determined, there would not be a third.

"Angelique?"

Garrett held the door to the carriage open, waiting to help her inside. She accepted his hand and stepped up into the coach. Within moments, the hackney lurched forward, and they were on their way to the wharf. Positioned beside her stepsister, Angie could hear Paden's horse following them.

They arrived at the docks and, familiar with the procedures of loading and boarding, Garrett immediately located the ship on which he'd secured passage, commissioned uniformed stevedores to man the trunks. His own belongings, he informed them, had been stowed earlier.

"I guess we're ready to board."

"Will the ship leave tonight?" Angie asked.

"No, tomorrow morning, but Paden and I thought it was best if we settled into our cabins early. A mere safety precaution, considering the situation."

"This is terribly exciting," Veronica remarked.

"I'm glad you think so, Madame. Let's hope your enthusiasm rubs off on Angelique."

Glancing off in the distance, Angie viewed the gentle rise and fall of the tall-masted clipper and already she could feel her stomach begin to churn. She swallowed. "The Oriental Hotel would do nicely for tonight, I think." From behind her, Paden's soft chuckle wafted to her ears. She spun on her heel. "I've changed my mind. I'm not going."

"But our passages have been paid in full," Veronica said, while Angie stared up at Paden. "This is the only way to avoid possible danger."

Angie's pleading gaze remained locked with Paden's dark eyes. "You cannot change your mind, *mi amada*. We have an agreement, remember?"

"But—"

Paden shook his head, whispering, "You promised."

Garrett cleared his throat. "We're wasting time."

At that precise moment, a shot rang out, splintering the night air and sending a shiver of terror down Angie's spine. She heard Veronica gasp, heard a man's voice shout, "Get down!" Then one moment she was on her feet and the next she lay face down near a brick wall in front of which stood a row of barrels. She lifted her head and found Veronica in a similar position. Both Garrett and Paden were sprawled out beside them, guns drawn.

"You ladies all right?" Garrett asked.

Stunned, Angie nodded. Veronica did the same.

"See anything, Garry?"

"Nothing. But I think it came from behind that warehouse."

"I think so, too." Paden sighed wearily. "If the gunman is Rosewahl's son, I am the one he wants to kill, not the rest of you." He paused. "Garry, cover my back while I make my way to my horse. I'll ride off, and hopefully our assailant will follow. After I'm gone, you three make haste and get on board the ship."

"Sounds good," Garrett agreed.

"But your arm, Paden."

"It is all right." He turned slightly to face Angie and gave her such a long look that she wanted to cry. Glancing back at Garrett, he said, "Ready?"

"Ready."

"I can't watch," Angie murmured, pillowing her head on her arms. Next to her, she felt Paden rise and heard his boots as he ran along the dusty, brick-lined alleyway that paralleled the succession of warehouses on the wharf. Then gunshots. More gunshots. The sound was deafening, and Angie had to cover her ears.

"Dear Lord, please keep him safe," she prayed aloud. "Don't let him die, please don't let Paden die. I'll keep my promise. I don't care if I have to be seasick for six months straight. Just please let Paden live."

The acrid smell of gunpowder filled her nostrils, and then the shots faded into the distance.

"Whoever's out there is definitely after Paden," Garrett said. He stood and hoisted Angie and Veronica to their feet simultaneously. A smattering of spectators had begun to gather on the piers that jutted out to assorted vessels.

"Come on, ladies," Garrett said, brushing the dust from his trousers, "we need to board our ship."

seventeen

"What about Paden?" Angie asked as Garrett ushered her and Veronica up the gangway and onto the clipper. The sun had set and now the stars twinkled overhead in the inky-black sky.

"Paden will be fine."

"But I'm worried."

Garrett paused on the deck. "This is typical for my cousin, Angelique. He's a gunfighter involved in some sort of risky business. He enjoys it. That's his vocation. That's his life. Now, mind you, I'm thankful he is a Christian," Garrett continued. "I no longer have to concern myself with the condition of his soul. But I'm sorry that my cousin has had time to work his wiles on you, my dear. Paden charms the ladies everywhere he goes."

"He did not work his wiles on me," Angie said, angrily pulling her elbow from Garrett's grip.

He gave her a sympathetic little smile before glancing at Veronica, who watched the exchange with an interested expression. "I think it would be best if we found our cabins," Garrett said at last.

"Good idea, Captain," Veronica replied.

He smiled kindly. "On this voyage, it would be best if you didn't call me 'Captain.' It may confuse other passengers. Besides, after this journey, my seafaring days are over. I sold the *Jubilee,* even in her sorry state, and I'm looking forward to a new life as a landlubber."

"Really? How very interesting. What will you do?" Veronica asked.

"I plan to stay in the shipping business, but I'll work in the offices with my father and grandfather instead of sailing around the world."

"Won't you miss all the excitement of the sea?" Veronica queried further.

Garrett chuckled. "I should say not. In many ways, my cousin and I are alike. We have remained unmarried so we could see what we wanted to see and do what we wanted to do. For myself, I have seen and done all I care to. It's high time for me to take a wife and settle down."

Angie purposely avoided his gaze as Garrett led them below deck and through an elegant central salon.

"My, but this is quite impressive," Veronica remarked, looking around the room with its mahogany woodwork, trimmed with polished brass.

Angie nodded, thinking this vessel seemed a far sight better than the schooner on which she'd sailed coming into San Francisco years ago.

"Just look at this long table," Veronica added. "And matching benches. . .is this where we will dine, Captain—I mean, *Mr.* Witherspoon?"

Again, he gave her a warm and patient smile. "Please call me Garrett. All three of us are practically old friends. But in answer to your question, yes, this is where we'll dine."

"And these doorways?"

"They lead to cabins, Mrs. Huntington," Garrett said, opening one of the doors. "Here's ours."

"Ours?" Angie asked, suddenly alarmed.

Garrett looked mildly chagrined. "It's the best I could do on such short notice. It's a cabin with a servant's quarters, but I think we'll be quite comfortable. Come, take a look."

Uncertain, she walked through the threshold behind Veronica and saw that the cabin was actually two rooms with a doorway dividing them. The first room, intended for a servant, was very small indeed, and had one berth. However, the second room was more spacious, having two berths against the porthole wall.

"This is fine, Capt—oh, I meant to say Mr. . .I mean, Garrett." Veronica blushed over her stammering. "And you must call me by my given name."

He chuckled. "Very well." He glanced at Angie. "Are the arrangements to your liking, my dear?"

"They're very appropriate, yes. Thank you." She noticed their trunks had already been delivered and, upon further inspection, decided this cabin would do nicely.

"There won't be a meal served tonight since no other passengers are expected to board, so I thought we could hire one of the crew to fetch us dinner from one of the restaurants in town."

"That sounds wonderful. I'm famished. How about you, Angelique?"

"Yes, I'm all for the idea. But I wonder," she said, turning to Garrett, "is it possible to find out if Paden is safe?"

He sighed, looking somewhat annoyed. "I think it's best if you forget about Paden."

Veronica stepped forward. "Cap—I mean, Garrett, I know Angelique will fret all night long unless we at least *try* to accommodate her." She smiled sweetly. "Please?"

He momentarily considered the request. "All right. I'll see what I can do. At the same time, I'll arrange for our food to be brought in."

"Thank you," Veronica replied. "You're very kind."

With a parting nod, he left their room. He traipsed through his own, entering the salon and closing the main door behind him.

"That man is incorrigible!"

"No, he's not, Angelique. He has been so helpful. What would we have done without him this afternoon?"

Angie didn't think she could rightly argue the point; Garrett had been extremely solicitous to both of them.

"And didn't he manage a gun well?" Veronica exclaimed, her hazel eyes brightening. "It must have been due to all his military experiences. Nevertheless, I felt ever so safe and protected. My, but we've had an awful amount of excitement these past two days, haven't we?"

Angie had to grin at her sister's rambling.

"Well, come and see what I bought for you this afternoon," Veronica said, unlatching the sturdy leather straps of one of the steamer trunks. "It's a gift."

"You shouldn't have, Veronica."

She shrugged. "I love presents, you know. So I bought us each a journal in which we can record our daily adventures—beginning with today's."

Angie took the proffered book. She liked to read, but didn't enjoy writing. Regardless, the gesture was considerate on her sister's part. "Thank you."

"You're very welcome. And look what else I purchased."

Angie glanced into the drawer of Veronica's steamer trunk. "Dime novels!"

"Yes. I bought penny dreadfuls by the dozen!" She laughed like a girl.

Angie shook her head. "Sister dear, these books are beneath us. We should be reading Charles Dickens or Nathaniel Hawthorne."

"Oh, what fun is that? I adore wild escapades. And just think, Angelique, we've lived through some of our own. We've traveled across the country by wagon train, and now we're sailing the ocean from coast to coast."

"Yes, I suppose we have seen our share of adventure." Angie couldn't stifle her smile.

"I should say so. Perhaps we should write our own dime novel." Veronica set her leather-bound journal on the lower of the two berths. "Since you're younger, you sleep on the top."

Still chuckling over the remark about writing a novel, Angie agreed.

"And you're not feeling the least bit seasick, are you?"

"Amazingly, no, but we're still docked. I only pray I feel good once we set sail."

"Pray. . ." Veronica paused. "You know, Angelique, it's been a long time since I prayed for anything."

Startled by the admission, Angie couldn't imagine her stepsister ever petitioning God for anything. "When was the last time you prayed?"

Veronica grinned. "Just this morning, actually. When Mr. Montano and the capt—I mean, Garrett—announced their plan to whisk you away from San Francisco, I begged God not to allow it. Then, after I realized there was no viable alternative, I prayed I could go along. Before this morning, I hadn't prayed since the day I married Billy. I didn't want to marry him, you know. My father forced me into wedlock."

Angie grimaced.

"I asked God to somehow stop the ceremony, but He didn't. After that day, I gave up asking God for anything."

"Until this morning."

Veronica nodded. "Until this morning."

Angie stepped toward her. "Sister dear, I imagine God heard all your prayers, but I have learned that His ways are higher than our ways and that the Lord can use those unexpected, unexplained tribulations in our lives. Sometimes we don't know why He has allowed such trials for us to bear, and perhaps it's not for us to ever understand. We just need to trust Him."

"Coming from you, Angelique, I might believe it's true. You have suffered as much as I, if not more."

"But there was a reason for my suffering, one being that I became a Christian during those dreadful years in Silverstone. God knew I had to reach the depths of despair before I realized my need for His salvation." Angie paused, considering her stepsister for a long moment. "What about you, Veronica? Are you aware of your own need for salvation?"

She shrugged. "I'm not sure what I believe. Can there really be a heaven and a hell? Can hell be any worse than what I've lived through with my late husband, that scoundrel?"

"Of course it can. The Bible says it will be much worse."

Veronica waved a hand in the air. "Let's not talk of such things. This is an exciting, happy time for us, Angelique. We're about to embark on a new life in New York City, although, I must admit, our life in San Francisco these past years has been quite comfortable. Still, I never cared for California and all the boomtown trash who have taken up residence in the state because of the mining prospects."

Angie nodded, sensing the moment to witness for Christ had vanished. Walking to her own trunk, she opened it and began to unpack a few necessities. Veronica did the same. Shortly thereafter, Garrett returned and announced that their supper had arrived; they would eat in the salon.

Taking a place on the bench beside her stepsister, Angie helped herself to the flaky, white rice, boiled fish with lemon sauce, and buttered carrots. Garrett sat across from them and chatted amicably about how this vessel differed from his own *Jubilee.* He admitted he would miss her, saying his ship had been his prized possession for years, but now he looked forward to starting anew.

"How ironic, Angelique and I just discussed that very thing. While we are grateful for our years as successful shopkeepers, we're excited about what lays ahead of us."

Angie merely smiled at Veronica's comment, but inside, she struggled to trust the Lord with her future. Did it include Paden? Was he safe? Had he reinjured his arm? She hoped she'd see him again. Amazingly, it saddened her greatly to think she never would. Did that mean she loved him?

The answer, she knew, was in placing her entire being in God's faithful hands. He knew the plan for her life, and He would reveal it to her in His good timing.

❧

The next morning, the sun streamed through the porthole as Angie and Veronica dressed. Angie felt a touch woozy from the all night rocking of the ship, but managed to change from her white cotton nightgown into a two-piece, tan walking dress with flounces and buttons adorning the front. Veronica donned a beige and white plaid gown with yarn tassels. Comfortably attired, they knocked on the adjoining doorway. Hearing no reply, they stepped into the smaller cabin and found it empty. Entering the salon, they spied Garrett at the long, mahogany table, sipping coffee and reading the newspaper. Seeing their approach, he wiped his mouth with a napkin and stood.

"Well, good morning, ladies," he said exuberantly. "And a fine morning it is to set sail."

After politely greeting him, Angie and Veronica seated themselves on the benches across from him. Garrett offered them warm, frosted, raisin biscuits that he had procured from a nearby bakery.

"Why, thank you," Veronica said, helping herself to one of the doughy treats. "You are the most thoughtful man I have ever known."

Garrett seemed taken aback by the candid remark. "I was brought up to revere any woman under my care. My father and grandfather were good examples to me."

"Oh, I'm sure," Veronica replied. "I merely find it. . . refreshing, is all."

Garrett grinned slightly, then looked at Angie, who quickly lowered her gaze. *Lord,* she prayed, *please let him fall in love with Veronica and not me. Garrett doesn't "revere" me—he wants to mold and shape me into his own little puppet.*

Angie picked at her biscuit, thinking that Garrett was as handsome as a man could be, with his walnut-colored hair and hazel eyes, his broad shoulders and tall frame. His very presence seemed to fill the entire salon and, while Veronica seemed woman enough to go toe-to-toe with Garrett, Angie felt suffocated by his commanding aura.

Polite chitchat ensued, but Angie remained silent throughout the remainder of the meal. Once they had finished eating, Garrett escorted them up the companionway to the deck, where they happened upon nothing short of chaos. Busy stevedores carried trunks onto the ship and called to each other while passengers boarded. Several people stood against the polished rail, waving to loved ones.

Angie searched the shoreline for Paden, thinking perhaps he'd want to say one last farewell, but her heart sank when his face didn't appear in the crowd.

"Witherspoon!"

Hearing Garrett's name, Angie swung around to see a stocky man in a blue uniform approaching.

"Well, well, if it isn't Jake Lancaster."

The other man removed his cap, revealing a balding head, and shook hands with Garrett.

Grinning broadly, Garrett made the appropriate introductions. "Veronica and Angelique Huntington, may I present Captain Jake Lancaster. We're old friends."

The man bowed courteously. "I hope you'll find your voyage comfortable, ladies. If not, please let me know at once so I may remedy the problem."

"Thank you, Captain," Veronica replied.

Angie smiled.

"You know, Witherspoon, I think it's quite unfair of you to keep such beauties to yourself."

Garrett smiled amusedly. "I am the ladies' chaperone. I'm a lucky man."

"I should say you are!"

Angie saw Veronica blush at the same time she felt her own cheeks warming in embarrassment. She glanced away, just in time to see Andy Stephenson striding up the gangway. He caught sight of her and smiled, heading in her direction. "Good morning, Miss Huntington."

She nodded demurely, feeling slightly suspicious. What did the man want? Did it concern Paden?

"I'm glad I arrived before your ship set sail," Stephenson said. "I have an important letter for you."

"Oh?" Angie took the proffered envelope, noting its wax seal.

"Yes, Paden asked me to deliver it. He said to tell you he's alive and well. One of my officers arrested the snipers last night. They turned out to be none other than Frank Rosewahl's son and a few of his friends. They'll have their day in court. Meanwhile, Paden has left town on business. I gave him my word that I would personally deliver his letter to you."

"Thank you," Angie replied. She felt so relieved to hear Paden was all right that she held the letter to her heart. "Thank you very much."

The police chief grinned wryly. "My pleasure. I wish you an enjoyable voyage."

Angie smiled, then watched as Stephenson made his way off the ship. Only then did she become aware of the three pairs of eyes staring at her. Chagrined, she excused herself and headed for the cabin, where she could read Paden's letter in private.

eighteen

Angie read and reread Paden's letter, thinking that if the ship hadn't already set sail, she might have changed her mind and gone ashore. Rising from where she'd been sitting on the berth, she walked to her trunk and placed the letter inside her Bible. Paden certainly had a way with words; his letter had warmed her heart and sent delicious tingles down her limbs. That man could charm the birds right out of the trees if he had a mind to. While Garrett continued to insinuate that Paden charmed all the ladies who crossed his path, Angie refused to believe it. It may have been so at one time, but Paden was a Christian now. Things had changed.

Remember your promise to me, Paden wrote. *I will not forget my promise to you. I could no more forget you, Angie, than I could forget the sun in the sky or my heart beating inside my chest. . . .*

Angie sighed dreamily. How utterly poetic. Placing her Bible on top of her trunk, she suddenly felt as though having Paden's promise in writing made it somehow official. Yes, she would wait for him, and the sooner she informed Garrett of her decision, the better. Perhaps he would finally give up his ideas of marrying her and set his cap for another woman—namely Veronica.

But she's not a believer, Angie reminded herself. Nibbling her lower lip contemplatively, she decided to take up the matter with the Lord. He was in the miracle business after all—and that's what this situation required: a veritable miracle.

❧

Paden struck a match and lit a small fire, then put the skinned rabbit on a spit across the flames. Sitting down on the rocky terrain, he glanced at his horse, which grazed on sparse clumps of grass off in the distance. Darkness was rapidly descending on the California desert, and somewhere off in the lonesome vastness, a wolf howled. Paden's horse snorted nervously. "Do not worry, *Medianoche*," he told the animal, "I will not let any harm come to you."

Returning his gaze to the campfire, Paden thought over the events of the day. Once more, he had uncovered nothing. Weeks had passed and still no trace of Munson. Paden hated to admit it, but he'd lost the man. Had he even suspected this outcome, Paden would have gotten on that ship with Angie. By now, she was probably somewhere in the South Pacific, nearing Cape Horn, her journey half-completed. Paden prayed for her daily, hoping Angie wasn't too seasick. He also prayed Garrett hadn't convinced her to marry him.

Paden turned the spit, reminding himself that if their union was meant to be, God would see to it that Angie waited for him. She had promised, and Paden planned to hold her to it.

❧

"Well, good morning, Angelique. It's good to see you out and about. You must be feeling better."

Looking up from her Bible, she smiled weakly as Garrett approached. "I am a bit better, thank you."

He looked out over the deck. "Calm seas, blue skies—a beautiful day."

Angie sighed, thanking God that the ship wasn't rocking to and fro as it had for the past two or three weeks. She had been holed up in her cabin, retching from seasickness for the duration.

"It won't be long now," Garrett mused aloud, taking a seat beside her on the bench that was firmly bolted to the deck. "We have about three weeks left to go, assuming the strong winds hold and we don't run into any more choppy weather."

"Perish the thought!"

Garrett chuckled, and Angie moved over to accommodate his girth. Then she noticed how tan his hands and arms appeared against his white shirtsleeves, which he'd rolled to the elbow. She looked up past his broad shoulders and saw his thick neck and face were sun-bronzed, and his dark brown hair now had golden highlights. He was as healthy as she was ill.

He met her gaze, and Angie averted her eyes.

"I think it might be a good idea if we disembarked in Brazil and let you recuperate," he said, leaning forward, his forearms on his knees, hands folded.

"But that will prolong our journey and you said you wanted to be home by Thanksgiving."

"True, but you're looking terribly pale and I don't think we should take a chance on you losing more weight."

Angie wetted her dry lips, suddenly ashamed of how loosely her dress hung from her shoulders. She had tried in vain to conceal her thin form.

"There'll be nothing left of you by the time we reach Maine."

Angie's head snapped up. "Maine? But Veronica and I planned to go to New York."

"Well," Garrett said haltingly, "plans have changed."

"But—"

"Now, Angelique, don't argue with me. Veronica and I discussed this matter a week or so ago and decided it would be best for the two of you to spend the holidays with my family and me in Maine. It doesn't make sense for the two of you to arrive in New York City and have no place to go. You can't very well land in a foreign city and expect to open a dress shop without the proper contacts."

She swallowed a retort, sensing he was right. "But Paden said—"

"Angelique, my cousin can track an outlaw through the desert at night, don't you think he'll be able to figure out you're in Maine?"

She cringed at his brusque reply and looked down at her Bible in her lap.

"Oh, I'm sorry," Garrett said. "Call me a sore loser. Call me whatever you want, but it displeases me greatly that you have chosen him over me. He can't offer you what I can. A life of comfort, befitting of a refined lady such as yourself, as opposed to hard work in the grueling elements on the range with a gunfighter. What are you thinking, Woman?"

"I'm thinking I'm not as 'refined' as you've assumed."

"Oh, not that again." With a derisive grunt, Garrett stood and walked to the rail and looked out across the expansive blue-green sea. "I sincerely hope you've prayed about this," he called over his shoulder.

She nodded. All she had done was pray about her promise to Paden, and the one thing God continued to reveal to her was that she could not go on living a life of pretense the way she had in San Francisco. With Paden, she could behave like the woman God created her to be: Angela Sarah Brown. Paden knew her innermost, darkest secrets, and he said he loved her regardless. Conversely, if she explained the truth to Garrett, she truly believed he would never understand.

She watched as he turned from the rail. "And this is your final decision?"

Again, she nodded.

"Very well, Angelique."

She lowered her gaze, fingering the silver-edged pages of her Bible.

With a sigh, he strode to the bench and sat down again. "I still think we should get off when the ship docks in Rio de Janeiro so you can get some rest."

"No," Angie replied, "I don't want to be a bother."

"You're no bother." He paused, before muttering, "Besides, my cousin will skin me alive if I release you from my care looking like an emaciated waif."

At the facetious retort, a swell of laughter bubbled out of Angie. Then, glancing at him askance, she decided she liked Garrett a whole lot better when he wasn't in love with her.

❧

Paden sat in a comfortable chair in Allan Pinkerton's Chicago office. He supposed he hadn't exactly failed his last assignment, since Munson turned up dead in a mining camp in Arizona. The desperado had apparently gotten himself killed after a heated card game. However, the money he stole would never be recovered, and Paden felt like he'd botched the job for the first time ever.

"Never mind Munson, that two-bit criminal. I've got bigger plans for you," Allan Pinkerton said in his Scottish burr. A stocky man with balding head and bushy beard, he had emigrated to America nearly thirty years ago in order to escape arrest for his part in aiding revolutionists fighting for workingmen's reforms. During the Civil War, Pinkerton had set up a secret service for the Union Army before going into business for himself. "I would like you to open some remote offices in the West and train my agents assigned out that way. You're quick with a gun, you know the land, the people, and the Indians."

Paden mulled over the remark. True, his arm had healed, so he was still quick on the draw. Nevertheless, he felt he couldn't take the job. "That is a generous offer, *Señor* Pinkerton, but I am afraid I cannot accept."

"I pay my agents well, and you know it—but I will double your salary."

Paden sat forward and rubbed his neck in indecision. The position sounded like a good one, and it would remove him from the manhunts he had grown to despise. However, he'd promised Angie no more gunfights, and he didn't think she would view this opportunity as an adequate compromise, let alone a godsend.

"I'm sorry," Paden said at last, shaking his head, "the job is not for me."

"Think about it," Pinkerton replied. "I'll give you twenty-four hours."

He grinned, knowing "The Eye," a name by which Pinkerton was commonly referred to, did not like to hear no for an answer. Paden stood and shook his employer's hand.

"I'll look forward to hearing from you," the Scotsman said with a knowing grin.

Paden gave him a parting nod and left the office. Walking the short distance to his hotel, he stopped at the front desk to check for messages. Days ago he had wired a Pinkerton associate in New York, hoping for word on Angie's arrival and whereabouts. So far there had been no reply, and Paden had begun to feel impatient.

"Yes, Mr. Montano, this came for you a short time ago," the uniformed young man said.

Taking the proffered slip of paper, Paden politely tipped his hat to the clerk, then stepped away from the desk to read it. After scanning the note, he crumpled it and shoved it into his jacket pocket. The ship had come and gone, but Angie and Veronica Huntington were not among the passengers who disembarked. Paden knew what that meant. Garrett had obviously managed to persuade the ladies to change their minds and travel to Maine. Well, that wasn't so bad, he decided, leaving the hotel and heading for the telegraph office. Maine had been the original destination. He only hoped and prayed his cousin hadn't cajoled Angie into more than rearranging her itinerary.

❧

Looking out over the ocean in the chilly November breeze,

Angie gripped the rail and watched as the clipper neared Maine's Casco Bay. It seemed so close, but the captain had said this morning it would be hours before they actually docked.

As she thought over her journey, Angie felt incredibly blessed to have fared so well on the last stretch up the Atlantic. Of course, two weeks in Rio de Janeiro had done wonders for her body and spirit. Since Garrett had been there several times, he had acquired just the right contacts to order the food they wanted to eat and arrange for travel to the sights they wanted to see—that is, the sights Veronica wanted to see. While Angie recuperated, Garrett had no choice but to escort and entertain Veronica on one adventure after the other. From the reports she'd heard from her stepsister, Angie could tell Garrett wasn't minding the company in the least bit. In fact, it seemed to Angie that Veronica and Garrett were falling in love.

Stifling a grin, Angie glanced to her distant right where even now the two stood engaged in some deep conversation. They made a handsome pair: Garrett in a crisp, white shirt, dove gray vest, black jacket, and matching pants turned into leather boots, and Veronica wearing her tartan plaid dress with its black velvet trim.

Just then the very object of her thoughts whirled around and, with tears in her hazel eyes, rushed past Angie. Garrett followed her, then stopped.

"What did you do?" Angie asked accusingly.

After a deliberate pause, he replied, "I merely stated the truth, Angelique." He turned to face her and his expression softened. "I suggest you go after Veronica and see if you can comfort her."

Angie nodded and strode quickly to their cabin. Inside, she found her stepsister standing with her head against the outer wall, weeping. "Oh, you poor thing, what's happened?"

"I feel like such a fool," Veronica said. Angie put her arms around her and Veronica cried on her shoulder. "I told Garrett I loved him. I couldn't help it. The words came out of my mouth as if by their own volition."

"I can hardly say I'm surprised by the admission."

"But, unfortunately, there is no happy ending to report. Garrett said a match between us isn't possible. I accused him of still being in love with you, but he said that wasn't the case." Veronica sniffed. "He–he led me to believe he had feelings for me," she stammered. "Oh, I knew all men were veritable beasts, yet I fooled myself into thinking perhaps Garrett was different."

Just as Angie felt her ire on the rise, she perceived the real dilemma. "He's telling the truth. I know what the trouble is. You see, there can't be a match between the two of you until you share Garrett's faith."

Veronica brought her head up, searching Angie's face. "Attending church is really that important?"

"It's more than just church attendance, sister dear. Salvation is all about seeing your need for the Savior, Jesus Christ, accepting Him and what He did on the cross, and having a personal relationship with Him."

With a sigh, Veronica stepped away and found her hanky. She dabbed the tears from her eyes. "Seeing my need for the Savior, hm?"

"That's right."

"And what, exactly, do I need Him for?"

"For eternal life in heaven. We're sinners and can't get there on our own." Angie wanted to be careful with what she said so that Veronica's decision to accept the Lord wouldn't be based on her love for Garrett, but on her love for God. "However, Jesus Christ died for you in the same manner He died for me. . .a sinner."

"Yes, yes, you've talked about sin before," Veronica stated impatiently, "and you said sinners can't go to heaven. But,

Darling, I am not a sinner. I haven't done anything wrong. All the wrongs have been done to me. Why did God allow me to suffer?"

Angie shrugged. "I don't know for certain. Perhaps He wanted you to see your need for Him. I know for myself that when things are sailing along smoothly in my life, I tend to forget about the Lord and how much I need Him to guide and protect me; but when I'm in trouble, He is the first one I call upon."

"My father used to say that religion was for weak-minded people who turned into hypocrites every Sunday morning."

"Yes, well, your father was a—" Angie bit her lower lip to keep from spitting out hateful words. She had long ago forgiven the man for the diabolical deeds he'd inflicted upon her innocence, but there were occasions when anger, bitterness, and resentment arose along with the unwanted memories.

Please, Lord, she prayed, *take these unrighteous sentiments away from me. Heal my heart, my spirit, as you have done so many times in the past. . . .*

"Angelique?"

Opening her eyes from her momentary prayer, she looked at her stepsister.

"You have every right to loathe and despise my father."

"Not in God's eyes, I don't. Jesus said hatred is the same as murder."

"Surely not."

"And murder is punishable by death. . .eternal death."

Veronica opened her mouth to retort, then closed it again. Spinning on her heel, she paced the room before turning back to Angie. "I hated my late husband."

"Yes, I know. You've told me so."

"I still hate him."

Angie nodded. She could tell.

"But you see, I thought Garrett would change all that. I

thought he would show me the love of a good man and dispel my unfavorable feelings for the male gender."

"Only Jesus can do that, sister dear. Not Garrett."

Veronica gave her a curious glance before Angie strode to her trunk and retrieved her Bible.

"Here, read the Gospel of St. John, chapter three. We can talk more afterwards."

Hesitantly, Veronica took the opened Bible and sat down on the lower berth. "I've never read the Bible before."

Angie gave her a patient smile. "I hadn't either, up until six years ago. My mother read it sometimes," she added wistfully. "Mostly just before she died. I had thought the Bible was for old and dying people, but I have since learned it's for all ages."

Veronica looked down at the Book in her lap.

"Will you read the chapter I've pointed out? I think it may answer some of your questions."

"Yes, I'll read it," Veronica promised. "I suppose it's time I find out what all this religion business is really about."

Angie smiled, then left the cabin, praying her stepsister would allow the Holy Spirit to show her the truth from God's Word.

nineteen

As it happened, there wasn't much opportunity to discuss spiritual matters with Veronica before having to prepare to disembark. However, Garrett seemed pleased with Angie's progress and promised to make time to address any further questions Veronica had once they were settled at his parents' home, located on the outskirts of Portland.

The ship docked and Angie, Veronica, and Garrett, along with all the other passengers, prepared to go ashore. Sunshine tried in vain to warm the crisp November day while the ship's canvas sails flapped noisily in the wind. The crew called to one another as the gangway was lowered, and soon people began to file off the deck.

Once on dry land, Angie's knees wobbled. If it hadn't been for Garrett's hold on her elbow, they surely would have buckled. A similar occurrence took place after they'd docked in Brazil. Angie realized Veronica was having the same problem. Garrett, on the other hand, being the seasoned sea captain that he was, found the matter amusing as he assisted both women into a hired carriage.

"You two rest," he said with a charming grin, "and I'll fetch our trunks."

Angie and Veronica replied with grateful nods. "I'm thankful the voyage has come to an end," Angie stated with a sigh, leaning her head back against the black leather upholstery.

"I'm rather disappointed," Veronica said. "I enjoyed every bit of our journey. However, I must say, I'm glad to be on the East Coast once again. I hadn't realized how much I truly abhorred San Francisco until I left the city behind me."

Angie smiled wanly, then closed her eyes.

"Will you miss it?"

Her eyes opening, she glanced at her stepsister. "Miss San Francisco?" Angie shivered and pulled her wool shawl more tightly around her shoulders. "I'll miss its warmer weather, that's for certain."

"It gets chilly in San Francisco, too."

"Yes, but not like this."

With her own shawl draped about her shoulders, Veronica shrugged. "Oh, what's a little cold weather that a cozy fire and cup of hot tea can't fix?"

"Wait until it snows," Angie muttered.

"Snow is lovely."

She shivered again.

Minutes later, Garrett appeared and the carriage rocked to and fro as the hired hands loaded the travelers' belongings on top of the vehicle. Then Garrett climbed in and they were on their way. As they bounced along the cobbled streets, he pointed out various sites of interest, such as Portland's college and a host of architecturally unique, red-bricked structures. He explained that a fire nearly twenty years ago had leveled much of the city.

Soon the buildings and houses grew farther apart as they left the bustling heart of town. Then Garrett pointed out his parents' home as the carriage made its approach. Peering out the window, Angie noted the house was square in shape and constructed with the region's ever-popular red brick. Nevertheless, it appeared to be a regal-looking estate, and Garrett boasted of the magnificent view of the Atlantic from its third floor observatory.

"I certainly hope we won't be an imposition," Veronica stated, wearing a worried little frown.

"Not at all. My family should be expecting us since I wired them when the ship last docked."

After the carriage halted in the circular drive, Garrett helped each woman alight. The front door swung open, and a stern-faced butler, primly attired in black and white, greeted them. "Master Garrett," he said, a slight grin curving his thin lips. "How good to have you home at last." He gave each lady a look of inspection before bowing courteously.

"Jarvis! My, but you're a sight for sore eyes." Garrett smiled broadly. "May I present the Huntingtons, Veronica and Angelique."

Again, the balding man bowed. "At your service."

"Please see to our things, Jarvis," Garrett instructed, "while I take the women inside before they freeze to death. They're accustomed to a warmer climate."

"Of course, Sir."

Garrett led Angie and Veronica into the large home, where a small reception awaited them in the foyer. After hugs and kisses from several ladies, Garrett received claps on the back from two males, one of whom resembled an aged version of Paden, and Angie stifled a little gasp upon seeing him. After introductions were made, she knew the reason for the resemblance; the man was none other than Alonso Montano, Paden's father.

"How wonderful to see you," Garrett told his uncle and aunt and two dark-eyed, female cousins, "but it's so late in the year for a trip from Mexico."

Glances were exchanged all around. "Garrett, Dear," his mother, Mary, began, "we've had a death in the family. Your grandfather. We tried to reach you after receiving your wire, but with no success."

"Grandfather is dead?" Garrett looked immediately stricken.

Angie's heart went out to him and the entire family.

"He died a couple of weeks ago, Son," John Witherspoon said. "I'm afraid you missed the funeral."

A shroud of sorrow descended on the little congregation.

"He died peacefully in his sleep," Paden's mother, Kathleen, said on a more positive note. "And he was eighty-nine, for pity's sake. No one lives forever."

"How true," John replied with a sad smile.

"We did reach Paden," Kathleen added. "He wired back to say he was on his way. We sent a return message telling him it wasn't necessary for him to make the journey. Unfortunately, we were told he had already left the hotel in Chicago."

"I suspect his arrival has to do with something more than just Grandfather's death." Garrett pulled Angie forward until she stood beneath Kathleen Montano's scrutiny. A lovely woman with dark brown hair, graying slightly at each temple, Paden's mother bore a striking likeness to her brother and Garrett. "Aunt Kathleen," he began again, "I think you and Uncle Alonso will want to get to know this lady."

"And why is that?" she asked curiously, her serious hazel eyes staring into Angie's.

"Because Paden has a mind to marry Angelique."

Gasps of surprise filled the elegant front hallway, and Angie felt her face flame with embarrassment.

"Well, Paden's wire suddenly makes more sense," John said with a huge grin. "He asked if someone named Angie had arrived, but we hadn't the foggiest idea to whom he referred. But now I understand—Miss Huntington, you are Paden's 'Angie.' "

"She is indeed," Garrett said, and Angie couldn't detect a single note of bitterness in his voice, for which she felt enormously grateful.

"I think my son has good taste in women," Alonso said with a thick Mexican accent. Smiling, he slipped his arm around his wife's trim waist. "His taste is almost as good as mine."

Angie felt her blush deepen.

Paden's sisters began speaking in such rapid Spanish, that Angie couldn't discern a single word. Their parents chuckled.

"My daughters both think it's about time Paden settles down," Kathleen translated with a hint of a smirk. "Two of his younger sisters are already married with children and Regina, here, is betrothed."

The ebony-haired beauty smiled shyly while her younger sister, Eva, gazed on with admiration shining from her dark gaze.

"This is quite the surprise," Mary said, her brown eyes searching her son's face. "And what about you? When are you going to get around to finding a wife?"

"I'm, um, working on it, Mother."

Angie glanced over just in time to see Garrett look at Veronica, whose cheeks now matched the crimson stripe in the foyer's multicolored wallpaper.

The butler came in from outside and offered to show Angie and Veronica to their room. "I hope you don't mind," Mary whispered as they started up the steps behind Jarvis, "but with all the Montanos here, you'll have to share a bedroom."

"We don't mind a bit," Veronica assured the older woman. "Angelique and I have been sharing a cramped cabin for months."

Mrs. Witherspoon looked relieved. "Thank you for your understanding."

"Thank you for your hospitality," Veronica returned, and Angie had the distinct feeling the two would get along very well.

❧

Paden watched from the train window as the picturesque landscape rolled by as if painted on a moving scroll. For all his musing, he barely saw it. Soon he'd arrive in New York, and if, after scouring the city, he didn't find Angie, he planned to wire his aunt and uncle once more. Why hadn't she been on that ship when it docked in New York, and why, if Angie hadn't disembarked there, wasn't she in Maine? Where else would Garrett take her? Yes, Garrett, his boyhood chum and favorite cousin—he was up to something. Paden sensed it.

He thought back to when they were boys, stirring up mischief in the streets of Portland. He recalled how their grandfather had showed obvious favoritism toward Garrett, acting as though he were almost ashamed of Paden. Always, Garry would share whatever trinket Grandfather had given him and, always, it was Garry who played the diplomat, saying things like, "Grandfather doesn't mean any harm, he's just old." When they got into trouble, Garry did the talking.

They grew and became young men and only saw each other every couple of years. Both Paden and Garrett had dreams of accomplishing more than the average man, but where Garry was a Christian and lived morally, thus dubbed "the good one," Paden experienced the darker side of life and, therefore, became looked upon by Grandfather Witherspoon as "bad blood." Even so, Garry continued to befriend Paden, risking Grandfather's wrath.

When the Civil War began, both Paden and Garrett enlisted. They kept tabs on each other and miraculously met up near the war's end. Garry persuaded Paden to take the train home to Maine with him, and Paden did. It was then that their grandfather's prejudice dissolved. At last, Paden felt accepted by his New England kin, although he knew he'd never fit into their family, their lifestyle.

Now Grandfather was dead. Paden felt a stab of remorse; he hadn't even told the old man about his conversion to Christ.

As he continued to reflect upon his life, thinking of his family, the Witherspoons, and specifically his cousin, Paden wondered if Angie wasn't better off marrying Garry. It was a heart-wrenching notion, yet it carried with it a ring of truth that Paden hated to realize. Once Angie glimpsed the Witherspoons' finery, an obscure, dusty ranch in Texas would no longer be appealing.

Even so, he had a promise to keep.

twenty

"Angelique, I cannot believe I'm doing this."

She laughed. "I can't believe you are either. Now hold still."

Veronica complied, and Angie continued to pin together the white, satin fabric. "Life can change so fast."

"I'll say," Angie replied in spite of the straight pins between her lips.

"It seemed as though one moment I was in San Francisco, a lost widow, despising the idea of remarriage, and the next thing I know, I'm a Christian here in Portland, Maine, getting fitted for my wedding dress."

Angie grinned. She still couldn't get over her stepsister's conversion. She never thought she'd see the day, but one Sunday afternoon, nearly two weeks ago, Veronica asked Jesus to save her. As a result of the pastor's clear gospel message that morning, all the knowledge about God swirling around in Veronica's head found a home in her heart.

Garrett had been pursuing Veronica ever since.

"I've never experienced such peace," she stated, "as I've felt since trusting the Lord. Although I have shunned the idea of marriage, I have peace about taking my vows with Garrett. As you know, Angelique, it's one thing to love a man and quite another matter entirely to spend the rest of your life with him, but God showed me something remarkable from His Word."

Angie's smile broadened.

"It was in the Gospel of Matthew," Veronica went on, "I memorized the verse.

" 'For this cause shall a man leave father and mother, and

shall cleave to his wife: and they twain shall be one flesh? Wherefore they are no more twain, but one flesh.' Aren't those the most beautiful words you've ever heard? Two hearts joined as one, and God created it." Veronica sighed dreamily.

Angie nodded in agreement. "But I feel badly for you," Veronica stated with a frown.

Removing the pins from her mouth, Angie looked up from her kneeling position. "Why?"

"Well, all along I thought you would be the one to get married and leave me to plod through life on my own. Instead, it's me doing the very thing to you that I balked at and resented."

"Don't worry about me. Paden will come for me. He promised." When no response was forthcoming, Angie stood. "He promised, and I believe him."

"But, what if—"

"Don't say it. We could 'what if' all day and accomplish nothing."

"True, except circumstances might arise that are beyond your control. You heard Garrett last night. Paden is a gunfighter. Gunfighters can get hurt. . .killed."

"Veronica, why are you trying to discourage me? Paden's parents seem to like me. I get along with his two sisters. They all believe that if Paden said he'd come, he'll be here. In fact, they're so sure of it, they've postponed their return to Mexico. Besides, Paden asked me to wait until Christmas. I can at least do that, can't I? Tomorrow is Thanksgiving Day. That gives Paden more than a month."

Veronica shrugged slightly.

"And the Witherspoons have offered their hospitality to me for that length of time, so it's not as though I'll be destitute and on the street after you and Garrett marry." She resumed pinning the satiny material together. "If, after Christmas,

Paden doesn't arrive, I'll put my name in at various dress shops here in Portland or even in New York. I'll find work." Angie wondered at the despair that filled her being after she'd spoken those words. Somehow, she couldn't bear to think of a future without Paden. Did that mean she loved him?

Again, Veronica didn't reply and Angie sensed there was something more troubling her stepsister. She ceased her pinning. "What is it, Veronica? Tell me."

"I feel awful," she said.

"Why? You're getting married to a handsome, wealthy man who adores you. Why should you feel awful?"

"It's twofold, really," Veronica confided. "First, I wish you were marrying a handsome, wealthy man who adores you, too, and secondly, I. . .I. . ." She swallowed hard. "I have a dreadful feeling Garrett still loves you."

"Hm. . ." Angie gave the notion a moment's thought. "Well, perhaps he does," she finally replied, grinning at the startled look on stepsister's face. "But it wouldn't be the same love he feels for you."

Veronica's expression relaxed a bit.

"If Garrett still loves me, it's a protective, older brother, perhaps even paternal love. That's not to say he wasn't infatuated with me at one time, but I believe those feelings have passed. He's realized that marrying me wasn't God's will and he's accepted it and moved on. I find that quite admirable, don't you?"

"If that's the truth, yes."

"Ask him," Angie said on a challenging note.

"I could never question Garrett about such a thing."

"I think you should. If you share your feelings with your fiancé, he'll share his heart with you, and your relationship will deepen."

Veronica grew momentarily pensive, then smiled. "How did you ever get to be so wise?"

Angie laughed. "I'm not, really. In fact, if I'm ever in your position and a bride-to-be, I'm sure I'll be running to you for advice."

"I hope you do, Darling."

"I will," Angie promised.

❧

Paden searched New York City and, as he suspected, Angie was nowhere to be found. According to plan, he wired his relatives in Maine. Their reply alleviated his worries about Angie, since it seemed she had arrived safely, but at the same time, the message caused his heart to plummet.

> *Angie here* STOP *Garrett to marry soon* STOP *Please come* STOP

So, she decided to marry Garry after all, Paden mused, pacing his hotel room with angry strides. *She promised me she would wait, but she goes back on her word. If she is that kind of a woman, then I don't want her and Garrett is welcome to her!*

After a few more furious thoughts, he paused and realized he didn't mean a single word of any of them. Yet, this was exactly what he had figured would happen. Angie discovered Garrett could offer her more, and what woman wouldn't choose a life of comfort in a cultured city over a life of hard work in the untamed West? He couldn't blame her.

A wave of self-pity stole over him, and Paden considered contacting Allan Pinkerton and inquiring after that last job offer. He had turned it down, expecting to marry Angie and buy a ranch. But what good would owning land be without a wife. . .without Angie? These past months without her had amazingly caused him to love her more. But now. . .

He lowered himself onto the edge of the bed, feeling as discouraged as the prophet Elijah had been when he lay down under the juniper tree. *Take my life, Lord. What good am I, a no-account gunman?*

In the next moment, it was as though the Lord God spoke directly to Paden's heart. The words were not audible, but more like an impression stamped upon his spirit. *Stop feeling sorry for yourself and board the next train to Portland.*

"Was that a command, Lord?" Paden asked aloud. "And if so, what would You have me to do once I arrive?"

No answer followed, but Paden felt sure God was directing him to take those first few steps. With renewed determination, he shook off his despair, packed his belongings, and headed for the train depot.

❧

The first days of December brought a snowfall, and the landscape looked as white and lovely as Veronica did in her wedding dress. It had been decided that Garrett's best friend and his wife would stand up as witnesses, and Veronica feared that Angie would feel hurt.

"You should be my bridesmaid," she had insisted, time after time. "I just wish I could make Garrett see my point of view."

"Not to fret," Angie replied. "Garrett explained his reasoning and I can accept it. He and this couple have been friends since elementary school, and over the years they prayed for Garrett's future spouse. They're delighted he has chosen you, sister dear. They should be in the wedding party, not me."

"Oh, Angelique. . ."

"Now, now," she warned, "a good wife must heed her husband's decisions without complaint."

Veronica grimaced, causing Angie to laugh, and once more she rejoiced in the fact that she wasn't the one marrying Garrett Witherspoon.

❧

The day of the wedding was frosty and cold. The sky looked

gray and mean. However, an air of excitement crackled within the confines of the cathedral walls in which the Witherspoons worshiped.

Sitting beside Paden's family in the long, polished front pew reserved for Witherspoon relatives, Angie smoothed down the skirt of her blue taffeta gown with her white gloved hands. At that moment, the organ began to play. Paden's youngest sister, Eva, sitting to Angie's right, looked enamored by the procession until finally the bride and groom stood before the altar.

"*Bella*," Eva whispered. "She is so beautiful."

Angie nodded in agreement. She had never seen a lovelier bride than her stepsister. The lacy, white veil added a touch of mystery and romance. Angie felt glad she had convinced Veronica of that wonderful moment when Garrett would unveil the face of the woman beside him and kiss her, his wife.

The pastor began to speak, but suddenly a disturbance in the back of the sanctuary caused stirs and whispers to waft across the large congregation. "Stop the wedding!" came the sharp demand. "I am sorry, but I cannot let you do this."

Shocked, Angie felt her blood run cold upon hearing the man's familiar, strong, smooth voice with its subtle accent. Next she heard his booted footfalls echoing through the church as he strode up the aisle. She turned and saw Paden standing not ten feet away. He looked quite dapper in his formal, black garb, and Angie's heart melted at the sight of him.

To her left, Kathleen Montano gasped and tried in vain to get her son's attention. "What is he doing?"

"I. . .I don't know," Angie replied.

Sitting beside Kathleen, her husband began to whisper something in Spanish and Angie distinctly heard the word "*loco*."

"Ah, if it isn't my favorite cousin," Garrett drawled with

a huge smile. "I had hoped you'd make it to town for my wedding."

"*Sí,* I made it. I always keep my. . .*promises*."

Angie inhaled sharply and raised her gloved hand to her lips, suddenly realizing Paden thought she was Veronica. No wonder he looked so angry. "Oh, dear," she murmured softly.

Just then Veronica lifted her veil, uncovering a curious frown, and Angie thought the expression on Paden's face was priceless. It went from shock, to confusion, to utter chagrin.

Angie began to laugh softly.

"Why don't you have a seat," Garrett said, looking amused and pointing in the direction of the Montanos and Angie.

Paden wheeled to his left, and when his dark gaze met hers, Angie didn't know whether to continue laughing or weep for joy.

Bowing courteously to the bride and groom, Paden publicly apologized for interrupting the ceremony before making his way to the pew.

"Scoot over, *chica*," he said softly to Eva, who did as he bid her, but not without tossing him an indignant glare. Obviously the young woman didn't appreciate being referred to as a "girl," even if it was by her older brother. He then placed a quick kiss on his mother's cheek before sitting down beside Angie.

Her heart pounded so hard, Angie was sure Paden would hear it. She threaded her hand around his arm and squeezed it, knowing the gesture would have to suffice for the embrace she longed to give him. With his right hand, Paden covered hers.

"For days I have been under the assumption you were marrying Garrett," he whispered so closely that she felt his warm breath on her cheek. "I was heartbroken, but then I decided I would make you look into my eyes and tell me you loved him more than me. Only then would I be satisfied. Only then would I step aside and allow you to marry him."

Angie shook her head. "I keep my promises, too, Paden."

He grinned and his dark eyes shone with affection. "So I see."

❧

After the wedding ceremony, family members and guests were invited to a reception at the Witherspoons' stately home. It wasn't until much later in the evening that Paden and Angie found time to sneak away from the crowd. Taking her hand, Paden led her away from the congested front room.

"Where are we going?"

"You'll see," he replied.

Showing her through the kitchen, where the temperature soared from hot ovens and hired hands busily prepared one tray of delectable hors d'oeuvres after another, Paden escorted Angie into his aunt's private tea room in the back of the house. Then he shut the lead glass-paned doors. The tiny room had been enclosed with matching lead glass-paned windows and beyond them, outside, stood tall, snow-laden evergreens.

"I have you alone at last," Paden said with a grin, stepping toward her.

"Behave yourself, *Señor* Montano," Angie warned half-heartedly.

He feigned a look of indignation. "I always behave myself."

Closing the distance between them, he slipped his arms around Angie's waist. She allowed herself to enjoy the feeling of being held in his strong embrace. "I hope you missed me these past months."

Looking up into his shadowed features, she nodded. "I missed you very much." With her palms resting on his upper arms, Angie slid her hand over the spot where he had been shot. "Did your wound heal all right?"

Paden inclined his dark head affirmatively. "And you? Have you recovered from your voyage?"

"Barely."

He chuckled lightly. "I will never force you to sail again. From now on, we will travel by stage or the railroad."

"*Gracias.*"

Paden smiled, but soon grew serious once more. "There is a matter of importance I wish to discuss with you."

Angie lifted expectant brows.

"While I was in Chicago, Allan Pinkerton offered me an outstanding position. I would be training agents and opening offices throughout the West."

Angie felt her heart sink.

"He offered to double my salary."

She lowered her chin, hoping Paden wouldn't see her tears of disappointment. "I thought you wanted a ranch," she said in a strangled, little voice.

"What do you want, *querida?* Tell me. I want to hear it."

Angie swallowed her emotion. "I want a husband who loves me, children. . .I want. . ." She returned her misty eyes to his dark, probing gaze. "Oh, Paden, I want you. I love you. But I can't marry a gunfighter. I can't. I know my heart, and it would break each and every time you left me for one of your assignments."

"Then I suppose it is a good thing that I turned down the job."

Angie glared at him. "You're toying with me. How could you?" She pushed against him, but Paden refused to let her go.

"This is not a game, Angie, but I have longed to hear you speak words of love. Can you blame me?"

She ceased her struggles, considering him, and concluding that beneath the rugged, *vaquero*-like exterior, beat the heart of a sensitive, perhaps even vulnerable man.

"Tell me again," he urged. "Tell me you love me."

Angie's heart warmed to the request. "*Te amo,*" she murmured in his native tongue, knowing she meant each word. "*Te amo.*"

"That is music to my ears," Paden replied as he gently touched his lips to hers.

"Excuse me. . . ."

Startled by the interruption, Angie stepped backward. Paden heaved a sigh of frustration before swinging around toward the doorway where Eva stood, grinning at the two of them. "What is it?" Paden asked.

"*Madre* says it's time to wish Garrett and Veronica farewell. They're leaving on their honeymoon."

"Yes, Paden," Angie concurred, touching his shoulder as he stood with his back to her. "We should see them off."

Paden nodded. "Very well. Tell Mother that Angie and I will be there shortly."

"*Sí,* I will do that," Eva said, closing the door once more.

Facing Angie again, Paden's features softened and he gave her a long look. "Will you marry me?" he asked. "Marry me, Angie, and I promise to love and cherish you for the rest of my life."

She smiled as happiness bubbled up inside her. "Yes, I'll marry you."

He pressed another kiss on her mouth, then on her cheek, her neck.

"Paden, you must stop," she admonished, although she wished otherwise.

He reluctantly complied. "When you are mine, Angie," he avowed, "I will have a lifetime to love you."

"And I, you."

Looking pleased, he looped her hand around his elbow and guided her to the foyer, where the newly married couple prepared to take their leave.

Stepping forward, Paden stuck out his right hand and Garrett clasped it. "After all that has happened between us, I hope we are still friends."

"Of course," Garrett replied, wearing an earnest expression. "You are more than my cousin. You are my brother—my brother in Christ."

Angie saw Paden smile broadly and then the men's formal handshake became something resembling an arm wrestling maneuver.

"Take care, and congratulations to you."

Garrett clapped Paden affectionately on the back with his free hand. "You, too, and, um, I imagine you'll be a married man by the time Veronica and I return from our trip to Europe."

"You had better believe it."

Veronica spun around and hugged Angie. "It's official? You're going to marry him?"

Angie nodded.

"I'm so glad." Veronica tightened her embrace. "I love you, Darling, and I promise to write."

Tears filled Angie's eyes. "I love you, too. Please say you'll visit me sometime. . .on our ranch."

"Mercy, no!" Veronica exclaimed, pulling back. "You must visit me here in Portland. I've had enough of the West to last me a lifetime."

"But, sister dear—"

"Perhaps we'll meet somewhere in between," Garrett suggested diplomatically, taking Veronica's elbow and drawing her right up beside him. "God willing, there will be ample time for us to discuss possible sites. But right now, my wife and I must be on our way." He gazed at Veronica. "My wife. . . those two words have an awfully nice sound to them."

Veronica smiled back adoringly.

Watching them, Angie sighed, feeling a swell of happiness mounting within her. She glanced at Paden, and reality struck: God had done exceeding abundantly above all she could ever ask or think. He had brought a man into her life who understood her, loved her, and one whom she could love in return. In the process, the Lord had made a way for her to escape her sorry past once and for all. With Paden at her side, Angie knew she could now brave the future with an unmasked heart.

A Letter To Our Readers

Dear Reader:

In order that we might better contribute to your reading enjoyment, we would appreciate your taking a few minutes to respond to the following questions. We welcome your comments and read each form and letter we receive. When completed, please return to the following:

Rebecca Germany, Fiction Editor
Heartsong Presents
PO Box 719
Uhrichsville, Ohio 44683

1. Did you enjoy reading *An Unmasked Heart* by Andrea Boeshaar?
   - ☐ Very much! I would like to see more books by this author!
   - ☐ Moderately. I would have enjoyed it more if

   ____

   ____

2. Are you a member of **Heartsong Presents**? Yes ☐ No ☐
   If no, where did you purchase this book?______________

   ____

3. How would you rate, on a scale from 1 (poor) to 5 (superior), the cover design?______________________________

4. On a scale from 1 (poor) to 10 (superior), please rate the following elements.

   _____ Heroine　　_____ Plot

   _____ Hero　　_____ Inspirational theme

   _____ Setting　　_____ Secondary characters

5. These characters were special because ______________________

____

____

6. How has this book inspired your life? ______________________

____

____

7. What settings would you like to see covered in future **Heartsong Presents** books? ______________________

____

____

8. What are some inspirational themes you would like to see treated in future books? ______________________

____

____

9. Would you be interested in reading other **Heartsong Presents** titles? Yes ❑ No ❑

10. Please check your age range:

❑ Under 18	❑ 18-24	❑ 25-34
❑ 35-45	❑ 46-55	❑ Over 55

Name ____

Occupation ____

Address ____

City ____________________ State ____________ Zip ____________

Email ____